JINGLE-BELL
BABY

JINGLE-BELL BABY

BY

LINDA GOODNIGHT

First published in Great Britain 2009
Large Print edition 2010
Harlequin Mills & Boon Limited,
Eton House, 18-24 Paradise Road,
Richmond, Surrey TW9 1SR

© Linda Goodnight 2009

ISBN: 978 0 263 21195 5

Harlequin Mills & Boon policy is to use papers that are
natural, renewable and recyclable products and made
from wood grown in sustainable forests. The logging and
manufacturing process conform to the legal environmental
regulations of the country of origin.

Printed and bound in Great Britain
by CPI Antony Rowe, Chippenham, Wiltshire

To Denise and Ashley. I know you're reading this.
Love ya, my friends!

CHAPTER ONE

LESSON NUMBER ONE in birthing class: never drive a car cross-country alone. Especially during the ninth month of pregnancy.

But Jenna Garwood had never taken a birthing class.

For the tenth time in as many minutes, she cast an anxious glance in the rearview mirror, relieved to see that no one had followed her when she'd exited the interstate some miles back.

Since her escape from the Carrington Estate, she'd zigged and zagged from the east toward the west, careful to cover her tracks. After three days, she shouldn't be so worried. But the long arm of the Carrington family reached far and wide. And they didn't give up easily.

When she'd heard the plans they had for her unborn child, Jenna had done the only thing that made sense. She'd run.

She had always been weak, but the little girl beneath her breast had given her strength. After the humiliation and sorrow of the last two years, the baby had given her a reason to try again.

A moan slipped past a bottom lip raw from constant gnawing. She bent forward over the steering wheel to stretch the kink in her back wishing she hadn't spritzed the car's interior with eau de parfum this morning. The stench of dirt and oil intermingled with the honeyed notes of orange blossom rose from the floorboard like an unwanted visitor. Saliva pooled in her mouth. As she tried to focus on the road, she swallowed, regretful, too, of the hamburger she'd eaten for breakfast.

Somewhere in this empty Texas landscape, there had to be a quiet little town where she could rest…and hide…until the ache in her back subsided.

"Only a little farther, darling," she murmured to the hard ball around her middle. "Mommy's tired, too."

Tired was an understatement of monumental proportions.

Her back had hurt nonstop throughout the duration of her pregnancy but during the last twelve hours the discomfort had grown steadily worse. If it had been her belly instead of her back, she would have been scared.

In conjunction with long hours behind the wheel, stress was the likely culprit. She hadn't relaxed once since leaving the estate. Even sleep was accomplished with an ear to the door and her eyes half-open.

The stretching, pressing ache deepened. She really needed to find that town.

She reached for her handbag, a pink crocodile spy bag her mother had purchased for Jenna's twenty-second birthday six weeks ago. The purse, stuffed full of the very best cosmetics, a spa coupon, and a five-thousand-dollar shopping card, had been nothing short of a bribe and Jenna knew it. Unfortunately Mother never understood that monetary possessions had ceased to inspire loyalty in her daughter. Only one thing had her complete and utter devotion—the tiny person who, at this very moment, was causing a great deal of discomfort to Jenna's body.

As her fingers flipped open the purse flap, Jenna hissed a frustrated breath between her teeth. She no longer owned the elegant slider phone, complete with GPS and remote Internet access. Still fully charged and activated, she'd donated it to a bewildered but grateful soldier at an airport in Philadelphia. By the time the device had been located, it would be somewhere in the Middle East.

"Who would you call anyway?" Even 9-1-1 was fraught with difficulties. Though the Carringtons disdained public attention, choosing to deal with their scandals in a more discreet and private manner, Jenna would allow no chance of alerting anyone to her whereabouts.

She forced herself to breathe slow and deep. The tense, tense muscles in her back only grew tighter.

A flutter of panic trembled in her stomach. What if she went into labor out here alone?

She turned on the radio, praying for a distraction, while also pressing the car's accelerator. She needed to get *somewhere* fast.

A male voice, rich in Texas twang, came through the speakers to announce a fall festival at Saddleback Elementary School and a garage sale at 220 Pinehurst behind the Saddleback Pizza Place.

Saddleback must be a town. But where was it?

She gave the radio a pleading glance. "Can't you be a bit more specific?"

The pressure inside her body increased. A new and more insistent discomfort had moved around front to a spot low in her belly. Very low. She gasped and shifted sideways onto one hip. The pressure mounted, deeper, harder, stronger.

A guttural groan erupted from Jenna's throat. The sound was foreign, so different from her normal modulated tone.

From the radio pounded a driving beat of electric guitar and bass. The intensity echoed in her body.

The road ahead seemed to waver.

Fingers of iron gripped her abdomen. She was in trouble. Real trouble.

She blinked, panting, fighting the pressure. Sweat stung her eyes. Texas weather was cool, though not nearly as cold as a Pennsylvania November, and yet, Jenna was roasting inside the small blue economy. She reached for the air-conditioning controls and saw, with concern, how pale and shaky she'd become.

Before she could take another breath, a squeezing pain of epic proportions followed hard on the heels of the intense pressure.

"Oh no." She *was* in labor. Either that or her body was rupturing from the inside out.

Mouth open, panting like a puppy, she gripped

the steering wheel with both hands and tried to stay on the road.

"Not yet, baby. Not yet. Let me find a hospital first." She squinted into the glare of an overcast sky, hoping for something, anything. A town, a house, another car.

Nothing but the endless brown landscape and an occasional line of naked trees.

The pressure mounted again, little by little, a warning that another power punch was on the way. Dread tensed her shoulders. "Nooo."

Her body poured sweat. So unladylike. Had Mother perspired this much with her?

She had to escape the pain. She had to. Perhaps if she stopped, got out of the car and walked a bit. Walking had helped in the past to ease the back ache. Even if walking didn't help, she could drive no further. She wouldn't take a chance of having an accident.

She tapped the brake and aimed the car toward the grassy roadside. Her belly tightened again. With one hand, she grabbed for the rock-hard mound, moaning with dread. The terrible pain was coming again. She could think of nothing but the battle raging in her body.

Just before the agony took control, Jenna saw

a flash of barbed wire and orange fence posts. The fence moved closer and closer.

And there was nothing she could do about it.

As his King Ranch pickup truck roared down County Road 275, Dax Coleman had two things on his mind: a hot shower and a good meal.

At the last thought, his mouth curled, mocking him. He hadn't had a good meal since the latest of a long string of housekeepers quit two weeks ago. Supper would be microwave pizza or scrambled eggs, the extent of his culinary gifts. His own fault, certainly. He wasn't the easiest man in Texas to live with. Just ask his ex-wife—if you could find her.

A snarl escaped him. He reached over to raise the radio volume and drown out thoughts of Reba.

As he rounded the last lazy curve before the turnoff to the Southpaw Cattle Company, a car in the distance caught his attention. Dax leaned forward, squinting into the overcast day.

The guy up ahead was either drunk, lost or having trouble. Dax took his foot off the accelerator. The car, a dirty blue economy model, was taking its share of the road out of the middle. It wove to the left and then back again as the driver began to slow.

With a beleaguered sigh, Dax tapped the brake. He wasn't in the mood for drunks. He wasn't in the mood for any kind of people, come to think of it.

For the last five years, all he'd really wanted out of life was his son and his ranch. The rest of the world could leave him the heck alone.

The car ahead slowed considerably and aimed for the side of the road. Maybe the fella was having car trouble.

After an afternoon of helping Bryce Patterson separate calves, Dax was too tired and dirty to play nice.

Still, he was a Texan, and the unspoken code of the country was rooted into him as deeply as the land itself. Out here, folks helped folks. Even when it was inconvenient.

Another car might not come along for hours and cell phone usage was spotty. He grabbed the plain black device from the seat next to a pair of dirty leather gloves and a pair of fencing pliers. Sure enough. Not a single bar of connection. He tossed the phone aside.

"Don't know what good the blasted thing is if it never works where you need it."

As he glanced back up, still grumbling, the dirty

blue car wobbled off the road, onto the grass, and down a slight incline.

"Come on, buddy, stop. Stop!"

The car ahead kept rolling.

Five strands of brand-new barbed wire bowed outward before snapping like strings on a fiddle. Orange fence posts toppled. Dax's fence posts.

"Blast it!" he ground out through gritted teeth and slammed the heel of his hand against the steering wheel. Somewhere in the back of his mind he was proud of holding back the expletives that tempted his foul-tempered tongue like flirty girls. A few years ago, he would have let fly with enough curses to make the grass blush, but with a mimicking boy dogging his boot prints, Dax had cleaned up his act. At least, that part of his act. Nothing much would clean up the rest.

Braking hard, he slid the truck onto the shoulder and bounded out into a comfortable November afternoon. The metallic slam reverberated over the quiet countryside, joining the rattle and wheeze of the car now captured in his barbed wire like a sad little bluebird.

"Hey, buddy," Dax hollered, as he approached the still-settling vehicle. "You okay?"

His question was met with the slow, painful

screech of wire against metal, like fingernails on a blackboard. The driver didn't answer and made no effort to get out of the car.

Dax frowned, slowing his steps to assess the situation. Maybe the guy *was* drunk. Or maybe he was a criminal fixing to bushwhack an unsuspecting rancher. Dax considered going for the wolf rifle resting behind the seat of his truck but fought off the temptation. At six foot one and a hundred and eighty pounds, he could hold his own. Besides, he'd watched the car weave and wobble for a couple of miles. His gut told him something was amiss, either with the driver or the car. Maybe the guy was sick or something.

The car had been moving too slowly for any kind of serious injury so the accident was a by-product of another problem, not the cause. There had been no real impact other than the scraping entanglement with wire and the now-toppled fence posts.

"Blast it," he said again. No matter how tired he was, he'd have to get this fence back up in a hurry or risk having heifers all over the road by morning.

Slapping his Stetson down tight, Dax strode down the slight incline and across the narrow expanse of calf-high weeds toward the blue car. Other than a cloud of dust circling the tires and fenders, there was an eerie stillness around the vehicle.

Dax bent down to peer through the driver's side window. His gut lurched. The occupant was either a guy with really long hair or he was a woman. A real curse drifted through his head. He savored the word like chocolate pie. Women were a lot of trouble.

"Hey, lady." He tapped a knuckle on the glass while tugging the door handle with the opposite hand. "Do you need help?"

The woman was slumped forward, her head on the steering wheel. She was breathing, but her shoulders rose and fell rapidly as if in distress. Dax exhaled a gusty breath. Crying women were the second-worst kind.

Suddenly, the object of his concern arched back against the cloth seat. A cry ripped from her throat, scary enough to make him jump.

The sound shot adrenaline through Dax's veins. He yanked at the door. It was stuck. Strong from years of wrangling five-hundred-pound bovines, he yanked again, harder. The door gave way, digging up dead grass and dirt as it opened.

He reached in, touched the slender shoulder. "Miss. Miss, where are you hurt?"

She turned a narrow, haggard face in his direction. Her eyes were wide with fear. Dark blond hair stuck to a sweaty forehead and cheeks.

"My baby," she managed, the sound more groan than words.

"Baby?" Dax glanced quickly into the backseat, but saw no sign of a child.

The woman squirmed, her hands moving downward to her waist.

And that's when Dax knew. The woman with the wide, doe eyes and the teenager's face was in labor.

All the expletives he knew rushed to his tongue. Somehow he held them back, useless as they were to anyone but him.

"Talk to me, miss. How long have you been in labor?"

"The baby's coming."

The implication froze him solid. "Now?"

She managed a nod and then slid sideways in the seat, lying back against the opposite door. Her body rocked forward. She fought against it, battling the wave of pain he could see on her young face. Nature was taking its course.

Oh boy.

"I'm sorry," she said. "I'm sorry."

Sorry for what? Going into labor? Having a

baby? The latter set his stomach churning even harder. He knew about that kind of woman.

But he had no time to ponder the past or the woman's cryptic statement. His brain shifted into warp speed. He had a dilemma here. A real dilemma. A strange young woman was having a baby in a car on his property and he was the only human being around to help.

Great. Just great.

"We need to get you to a hospital."

Her eyes glazed over and she made that deep groaning sound again. His pulse ricocheted off his rib cage. He'd heard this particular moan before from cows and mares. The woman was right. They were out of time.

"All right, miss, take it easy," he said, as much to calm his own nerves as hers. "Everything will be okay."

She nodded again, her huge eyes locked on his face, clinging to his words, trusting him, a total stranger. Dax got the weirdest feeling in his chest.

"How far along are you? I mean, is it time for the baby?"

"Two weeks away."

Close enough to know this was the real deal. Dang. Dang. Dang.

"How long have you been in labor?" he asked again.

Her body answered for her. Dax was smart enough to know that contractions this close could only mean one thing. Birth was imminent.

Think, Dax, think. What did he need? What could he do, other than wait for the inevitable?

"I'll be right back," he said past a tongue gone dry as an August day.

She managed to lever up, almost heaving toward him. "No! Don't leave. Please. Please."

Her pleading voice ebbed away on the wing of pain, but not before the sound hit Dax in the solar plexus. What kind of jerk did she take him for?

Guilt pinched him. Okay, so he'd resented the interruption to his afternoon. He'd wanted to drive right past. The point was he hadn't. He might be a jerk, but he wasn't a complete slime-ball. Most of the time.

He touched her foot, hoping to reassure her. She was barefoot. A pair of fancy-looking silver shoes, complete with a perky bow, rested on the floor. He had the silliest thought that her feet were pretty. Slim and elegant like one of those ballet dancers.

What the devil was she doing out here alone?

"I need some things from my truck," he said. "It's right behind us. Not far at all. I'll only be a minute."

He loped to his Ford and dug out any- and everything he could find in the cab that might be of some use. There wasn't much, but he had an old blanket and plenty of water. A rancher could never be certain when he might be ten miles from the house and need water or a blanket. At least he could wash his hands and wrap the baby when it arrived. A bright-red bandanna on the floorboard caught his eye. Gavin had left it behind. Though the cloth was likely none too clean, he grabbed it anyway and drenched the soft cotton with water.

Back at the car, he leaned in to wipe the wet bandanna over the woman's damp forehead.

"It's me again," he said and then felt stupid for saying it. Who else would it be? The Seventh Cavalry?

The little mama made a small humming noise he took for gratitude. She must have been in between a contraction because her eyes were closed and her expression less tense.

As he straightened, he caught a whiff of some sweet-scented flower. Imagine, smelling like flowers at a time like this. She looked like a nightmare, but she smelled good.

He wondered one final time if he could toss her in the truck and get to the hospital in Saddleback in time.

Just as the thought flitted across his mind, her eyes flew open, distressed. "Oh, no. It's coming again."

She grabbed for his hand and squeezed with a grip that would have taken down a sumo wrestler.

"Easy now. Easy," he said, talking to her the way he would a first-time mare. What else could he do? He was no doctor.

All right, Coleman, he said to himself. You've delivered plenty of calves and foals. A baby can't be much different.

If he believed that he would have gone into the delivery room when Gavin was born.

"You're doing great. Long, deep breaths. Work with the pain, not against it." He didn't know where the advice was coming from, but she seemed to do better when he was talking. "Attagirl. You're doing good."

The contraction subsided and she dropped her head back again. Dax shared her relief. This baby-delivering business was hard work. His back ached from bending over the seat and his pulse pounded so hard against his eardrums, he thought he heard tom-toms.

Having long since tossed his hat aside, Dax wiped a sleeve across his forehead. Even with a cool breeze floating through the open door, he was sweating like a pig. But then, so was the little mama.

Drenched in sweat, her hair a wet wad around her face, she reminded Dax of a drowned kitten. Pitiful-looking little thing. Somebody, some-where was going to be real upset that she was out here alone on the Texas plains having a baby.

He wondered about the baby's father. About her family. She was young. Though her age was hard to discern at the moment, to an over-the-hill thirty-something like him she looked like a kid. She needed her family at a time like this, not some broken-down old cowboy with a bad attitude, who wanted to be anywhere but here.

She was a brave little thing. He'd give her that. Tough as a pine knot. She had to be scared out of her mind, young as she was, but she hadn't screamed or fought or carried on the way Reba had. She hadn't cussed him or the baby, either.

Dax tasted gall as the old humiliating memory thrust itself into his consciousness.

The little mama shifted slightly, emitting a murmur of dread. Another contraction must be on its way.

He gently rubbed her toes. She captured his eyes; a tiny smile lifted the corners of her mouth. Dax felt oddly heartened.

Here they were in about as intimate a situation as he could think of, and he didn't even know her name. What if something went wrong?

No, he wouldn't think of that. Even if his life was ruled by Murphy's Law, he was not going to allow anything bad to happen to this gritty little lady.

"Name's Dax," he said. "You feel like telling me yours?"

Something odd flickered behind pain-clouded eyes. She licked dry lips. Then her gaze slid away.

Before Dax could decide if her silence was fatigue or reluctance, the wave of nature took over again. As her shoulders rolled forward, straining, she whispered, "I wanted to be brave, but I'm so scared. Don't let anything happen to my baby."

The admission touched Dax somewhere in the cold lump he called a heart. "You're doing fine, little mama."

He wanted to say a lot of other encouraging things, to tell her how courageous he thought she was, but with the blood rushing in his temples and his gut twisting with anxiety at the huge responsibility before him, he just patted her pretty foot and muttered nonsense.

He didn't know how long he'd been there. Couldn't have been more than fifteen minutes though it felt like a lifetime when suddenly she gave one last heaving groan and it was over. She fell back against the car seat, her exhausted breathing loud in the quiet.

A baby, the smallest thing Dax could imagine, slipped into his waiting hands. He'd expected her to be pink and squalling the way Gavin had been. Instead, the tiny form was silent, limp and purplish.

His heart, already jumping and pumping to beat Dixie, rose into his throat. He glanced at the little mama and then down at the infant.

Please God, no. Not this.

CHAPTER TWO

THE BROWN-HAIRED BOY barreling across the yard of The Southpaw in cowboy boots and an open jean jacket lifted Dax's flagging spirits. The last few hours had been rough to say the least.

"Daddy!"

A swell of love bigger than his fifteen-hundred-acre ranch expanded in Dax's chest. He stopped in midyard and hunkered down. The sturdy little boy, smelling of pizza and backyard dirt, slammed into him. Small arms encircled his neck and squeezed.

Dax pressed the slender body to him, clinging to the thought that his son was alive and well. He didn't know what he would do if anything should ever happen to Gavin, a fact that had come home to him with a vengeance during these last few hours with the little mama.

Life was fragile. His thoughts flashed to the tiny newborn baby. Real fragile.

"Where you been?" Gavin was saying. "Rowdy had to stay a long time."

Dax looked up at the young ranch hand ambling lazily toward them, his usual crooked smile in place. Dax figured you could punch Rowdy Davis in the nose and he'd still grin. Sometimes the man's smirky cheer was downright irritating.

"Everything all right, boss?" Rowdy asked, clearly curious. "You were kind of short and not-too-sweet on the telephone. Had us worried some."

Short and not-too-sweet. Yep, that was him, all right. He'd simply told Rowdy to be at the house when the school bus delivered Gavin from kindergarten and stay there. Then, he'd hung up, too wrung out to explain that he was at the emergency room fifteen miles away with a strange woman whose baby he'd just delivered.

"Boys, do I have a story to tell. Let's get in the house first. I could use a cold drink." Since playing doctor on the side of the road, his appetite was gone but he still wanted a cold soda pop and that hot shower.

Gavin wiggled back from his embrace. "A story about Wild Bill and the buffaloes?"

"No, son," Dax said. "Not that kind of story."

He rose, lifting the five-year-old up with him.

Gavin looped an arm over his dad's shoulder and patted his opposite cheek. Dax felt that quivery feeling in the center of his chest. He didn't know what he'd done to deserve Gavin, but he was grateful. Without the boy, he would have given up on life long ago. As it was, he clung to the edges of hope, fighting off his own dark tendencies in an effort to give the motherless boy a decent upbringing. It wasn't easy. *Gavin* wasn't easy. And at times Dax no more understood the boy than he could understand Chinese.

A frown cut a deep gash between Gavin's black eyebrows. "It won't be scary, will it?"

Times like these. The boy was scared of his own shadow. Since hearing a ghost story at a fall party he'd been especially nervous.

"No, Gavin, it's not scary." He tried, but failed, to keep the annoyance out of his tone. The boy was skittish as a deer. The teacher had had to peel him away from Dax's side the first day of kindergarten. And Gavin had cried, an occurrence that both worried and embarrassed his father. A sissified kid wouldn't survive in today's mean world, but Dax didn't know how to change his child's disposition.

By now, they'd made the house and were inside. Dax tossed his hat at a heavy wooden end table, shrugged out of his jacket, and collapsed with an exaggerated heave onto a chair. The living room was enormous, compliments of his ex-wife who had insisted on a house big enough to entertain. Trouble was she'd done her entertaining while he was out working. He liked the house, though, liked the warm, golden-brown stone and wood fireplace and the wine-colored leather furniture.

He propped his boots on a squat ottoman. "You ever deliver a baby, Rowdy?"

Rowdy, who had ventured off to the kitchen, reappeared with a glass in hand. "What? Are you serious?"

Dax accepted the glass and gulped the icy drink in three long gulps. "Crazy afternoon. A young woman ran her car through my fence between here and Jake's windmill. I stopped to see what the problem was and she was having a baby."

Rowdy slithered into a chair, the grin forming a surprised O. "Man."

"Yeah. Tell me about it."

"Everything go okay? I mean, you delivered the baby and everything." As the reality of what Dax had done sank in, Rowdy leaned forward, elbows braced on his knees. "Holy smoke, Dax. Are they all right? The mama and baby, I mean?"

"The baby was kind of blue and not moving at first. I thought she was gone." Running a finger around the rim of the glass, he didn't mention how scared he'd been. The telling sounded a lot calmer than the actual event. "Then I thought about how calves are born with a lot of mucous sometimes, so I wiped her nose and mouth off with Gavin's bandana...." He patted the boy's knee. Gavin curled up next to him, listening to every word. "Just as I was getting ready to turn her upside down and swat her bottom, she let out a howl." Sweetest sound he'd ever heard.

"Man." Rowdy said again, seemingly devoid of intelligent comment. Dax understood. He'd been speechless himself at the time. As soon as the baby had cried, he'd wrapped her in the old blanket and made sure the mama was all right. Then he'd jumped behind the wheel of the car, forced the little economy onto the road and sped like a NASCAR racer to the emergency room.

"Where is she, Daddy? Why didn't you bring her home? I want to see her."

"She and her mama are in the hospital in Saddleback." He rattled the ice in his glass, shaking out a few more drops of cola.

Beneath a swatch of thick, dark hair a fretful frown puckered Gavin's forehead. "Are they sick?"

"The doc's going to check them over. But I think they'll be okay."

The child stuck his legs straight out from the couch and tapped the toes of his boots in a steady rhythm. "Noah's mama had a baby. They got to bring it home and keep it. Now he gots two brothers. But a sister would be okay, too."

Dax sighed. He and Gavin had this conversation every time one of the boy's schoolmates welcomed a new sibling. How did he explain to a five-year-old that his daddy wasn't the kind of man women wanted to have babies with?

"Is she from around here?" Rowdy's question gave Dax an excuse not to answer the boy. "The woman. Anybody we know?"

"No. Not even a Texan." He knew that for certain. Her buttery voice with its clipped syllables was upper-class Eastern, a Yankee. He'd stake his ranch on it. Even her clothes were different.

"What was she doing out here on a remote county road all by herself? Visiting someone?"

"Can't say." Though he'd been asking himself the same question. "We didn't exactly have a conversation."

"No, I guess not." Rowdy ran a thumb and fore-finger along his chiseled jawline. "What did she look like? Is she pretty?"

Dax shot him a frown. His top ranch hand liked the ladies and had a new one on his arm every week. Women seemed to like him right back. Still, the question didn't sit well with Dax.

"She was a scared kid." Scared but tough and courageous. He couldn't get that out of his head or the thought of the tiny, mewling baby that had been born in his hands.

"I'm sad for her, Daddy, if she's scared. Can we go see her?"

"I told you she's all right." The words came out a little harsher than he'd intended. Gavin blanched and sat back against the couch.

Dax patted the boy's knee, letting him know the sharp retort wasn't aimed at him. Gavin was tenderhearted to his old man's hard-hearted, plain and simple. But Dax refused to feel guilty about wanting the strange day to end here and now. He'd done his part to help the woman. He'd played the good Samaritan. She was re-ceiving expert care and the hospital would contact her family. He had a ranch to run and a downed fence to fix. He'd heard the last of the mysterious young mother and her baby. And that's the way he wanted it.

Jenna heard voices. She opened her eyes in a semidarkened room that smelled of antiseptic and oversteamed food. She faced a wall and a wide pair of windows covered by blinds. The morning sun sliced through, shedding strips of pale yellow across a white woven blanket. Memory flooded in with the sunlight.

The pain, the car, a tall, gruff-talking rancher with gentle hands.

"Oh." Her hands shot to her belly. The baby. The man had delivered her little girl and brought them to the hospital. A mix of embarrassment and wonder filled her. She'd had her baby in a car with only a stranger to help. Mother would be mortified.

She shifted in the narrow hospital bed. Her body was sore and stiff, but not painfully so, a fact that surprised her. After the torture in the car she'd expected to be half-dead today.

She rolled to her side, eager to hold her new daughter.

The baby was gone.

A tremor rippled through her as the possibilities played through her head. The nurses had left the newborn here, at the bedside, in an Isolette. Jenna was positive.

Had the Carrington machine already discovered her whereabouts?

Fighting the stiff sheets, she sat upright, only to tumble sideways onto the pillow, light-headed and weak. Blood roared in her temples. She took deep breaths, waiting until the black dots dissipated.

For a long moment, she remained still, frustration in every breath. Had someone recognized her and called her family? Was her baby girl even now in the smothering bosom of the Carrington clan?

The heavy wooden door opened with a swish. Jenna braced to face her censuring mother, determined to stand strong for her baby.

When a nurse appeared, backside first, Jenna wilted against the pillow in relief.

"Everything looks great with your little princess," the woman said, rolling the Isolette into the room. "Doctor checked her all out, gave her the requisite medications and said she was perfect."

"I didn't know where you'd taken her." Her voice sounded breathless and scared.

The nurse, a young woman with a long, black ponytail, whose tag read Crystal Wolf, RN, gave her a sympathetic pat. "Sorry, hon, you were sleepin' like a rock, so I didn't want to disturb you. Not after what you went through. You ready for her? Or are you too tired? You look a little pale."

Jenna held out her arms. Color would return now that she knew her mother wasn't on the premises. "Yes, please let me hold her."

"She's a darling. So pretty with all that fine golden hair and her little turned-up nose."

Jenna thought her daughter looked like an alien. A withered old lady alien. "Will her head always be pointed like this?"

With a shake of dangly white earrings, the nurse laughed. She reached over, flipped the soft pink blanket back and gently massaged the baby's head with a cupped hand. "You do that every day and before you know it, the cone head will be gone."

"Thank goodness." Jenna gave a shaky laugh.

She'd read books and searched the Internet on the topic of parenting and felt competent to be a mother, but now that the moment was upon her, the idea of caring for another human being frightened her. She had no home, no job, and no one to help. For a person who'd never been allowed to do anything for herself, she had a great deal to learn—fast.

"Do you have a name for this little princess?"

A gentle smile lifted Jenna's mouth. "Sophie. Sophie Joy because she is the greatest joy I've ever known."

"Oh, hon, that's beautiful."

Sophie stretched, her tiny face screwing up in an adorable expression. Jenna's whole body seized up with an overwhelming love, a love so powerful tears filled her eyes. This was why she'd run away. This precious bit of humanity deserved to love and be loved for the right reasons. She deserved to grow up free from fear and the hovering, controlling influences that had stymied Jenna's life since birth.

Her family, particularly Elaine Von Gustin Carrington, would not control this baby's life the way they'd controlled hers.

People who envied her opulent lifestyle had no idea what it was like to live in an ivory tower surrounded by hired bodyguards and nannies and private tutors. They had no idea the sadness of a child never allowed to play outside or with other children who were "not like us." They'd never sat with their faces pressed against the window watching others play in the snow while wondering what it would be like to build a snowman with someone other than a hired nanny and a burly bodyguard.

The world considered her a spoiled rich princess, but they were wrong. Elaine Carrington's elitism and her kidnapping paranoia had made her only daughter a lonely child, a prisoner of her family's enormous wealth.

Which was exactly the reason Jenna wanted Sophie Joy to grow up in a normal home, in a normal town, doing normal things. She'd play with other children and go to a real school and maybe even join a soccer team if she wanted to. When she was a teenager, she'd hang out at the mall and have sleepovers and attend school dances with friends of her own choosing.

Sophie would have a childhood her mother had only dreamed of, a wish that sounded foolish to most people—even her late husband, though he'd pretended something far different in the beginning. Early in their secret relationship, Derek had nurtured Jenna's longing to be a regular wife living in the suburbs. But the Carrington money had followed her in marriage, corrupting the boy who'd claimed to love her, and the few weeks of normalcy had disappeared as quickly as his love.

In the end, her mother had been right about her fortune-hunting husband, and Jenna had gone home to the estate, broken. From Derek, she had learned a cruel fact of life—never trust a man, no matter how pretty his promises. Men were only interested in someone like Jenna for one thing. As Mother had so succinctly put it, "A trust fund makes any woman attractive."

She swallowed back the festering hurt. She might not be beautiful, but she refused to care anymore. All that mattered now was assuring Sophie the happy, uncomplicated life and freedom she had never known.

To do that, she could never go back to the Carrington Estate or even to Pennsylvania.

As she marveled at her baby's velvet skin, at eyelashes so pale and perfect, the pink rosebud mouth, Jenna made a silent promise. No matter what she had to do from here, her daughter would lead a normal life.

The nurse, whom she'd almost forgotten, patted her arm. In a pleasant drawl she said, "I'll be back in a few, Jenna. We'll get your vitals again and then you'll be good to go."

Jenna's head snapped up. "Go?"

Go where? She'd hoped to stay in the hospital a few days, to get her thoughts together and form a plan. To read the newspaper and make sure the world hadn't been alerted to her disappearance. To figure out where to go and what to do with a newborn.

"Sure thing. Unless there are problems, an OB stays twenty-four hours or less these days. Would you like for me to phone your family?" The young woman reached for the chart at the end of the bed, flipped open a few pages. A frown appeared between her black eyebrows. "Seems we didn't get that information when you arrived yesterday evening. Well, it was a hectic time. No problem. Someone from the business office will be in. They always extract their pound of flesh."

Jenna managed a weak smile at the woman's joke. She hadn't thought about the hospital bill or even about the records a hospital would keep on her and Sophie.

She'd given them her name yesterday and no one had reacted. But she wasn't surprised no one recognized her face. Due to her family's paranoia, their only child had been publicly photographed very little. Jenna found a certain irony in that. The fear that had made her life a prison might be the very thing that assured her freedom. Unless her parents had released her disappearance to the press, there was a chance no one here in this small Texas town would ever guess that she was one of *the* Carringtons, reluctant heiress to a staggering financial empire.

"Would you like for me to call Dax?"

Jenna blinked. "Who?"

"The rancher who brought you in. Dax Coleman. I thought you knew him."

A warm blush crept up the back of Jenna's neck. She hadn't remembered her rescuer's name. "No."

"Oh, well, I just assumed…" The nurse flapped a hand. "Never mind. My mouth is running away, though it's too bad about Dax. He seemed real concerned, and for a reclusive guy like that, well, we just figured the two of you knew each other."

Was the nurse asking if she and Dax knew each other in the Biblical sense? Did she think Dax Coleman was Sophie's father?

Her flush of embarrassment deepened.

"Mr. Coleman," she said in her most dignified voice, "was kind enough to render aid to a damsel in distress. But no, I had never before made his acquaintance."

The nurse, who was darkly pretty and not much older than herself, looked disappointed. "Well, then, that's really too bad. Dax could use a spark in his life after what happened."

Jenna refused to ask the obvious question. "You know him?"

"Sure. In a region this sparsely populated everyone knows everyone else. Dax is an old friend of mine. Or used to be." The nurse fanned her face with her fingertips. "He's still pretty delicious-looking, too, if you know what I mean. Don't tell my husband I said that." She laughed.

Delicious-looking? Jenna remembered a gravelly, rough voice and strong, calloused hands, though he'd been as gentle as could be with her and Sophie. As far as his looks, she could only recall intense green eyes and dark hair that fell in sweaty waves onto his forehead. A cowboy. She remembered that, too.

En route to the hospital, he hadn't said much. But he'd glared at her and Sophie in the rearview mirror every few minutes until Jenna became convinced she'd somehow angered him. At the time, she'd been too tired and shaky to wonder about her roadside rescuer. Now she did.

"You were lucky he came along," Nurse Wolf said. "Out here you can drive forever and not see a soul."

She almost had.

"Yes, I owe him a debt of gratitude," Jenna

muttered, absently rubbing the side of her finger over Sophie's delicate cheek. She'd never been indebted to anyone before, ever. People were indebted to the Carringtons, not the other way around, but the cowboy, a total stranger, had been there for her and her baby when they'd had no one else. She wasn't likely to forget that.

"I'll be back in a few," the nurse said and started out the door.

"Nurse?"

The woman did an about-face. "It's Crystal. Please."

"Crystal," Jenna said, oddly pleased at the simple request. "Would you mind bringing me a newspaper or two?"

"Nothing newsworthy ever happens around here except church dinners and baby showers and school sports, but I'll bring you a paper."

The simple activities sounded like heaven to Jenna who'd never experienced a single one of them. "Thank you."

With a hand wave, Crystal sashayed out of the room, only to lean back into the room with a twinkle in her eye.

"Prepare yourself. A certain delicious cowboy is headed your way."

Jenna was sure her mouth fell open. "You're kidding."

But Crystal had already disappeared, leaving the door open.

Dax kicked himself all the way down the hall. He had no idea what he was doing here. He'd done the right thing already. He'd played the good Samaritan. He should be on the south side of the ranch right now fixing a water gap before snow or rain made the work miserable. But here he was at Saddleback Hospital in the maternity ward, feeling as uncomfortable as if he'd stumbled into one of those ladies' lingerie stores.

But he was here. Might as well get this over with.

Stetson in hand, he used the opposite hand to tap on the open door, doing his level best not to look inside until he was invited.

"Come in," a feminine voice said. He remembered that voice. Soft and educated and worried. He'd dreamed about it last night. Imagine that. Dreaming about a woman's voice. And her bare feet. And the way she'd gazed at him with trust.

Blast it. That's why he was here. She'd haunted his dreams and he'd not been able to get a thing done this morning until he was certain she and her baby were in good shape.

According to the desk nurse the baby he'd delivered was doing well. Thank God. That should have been enough. He should have turned tail and headed for his truck.

But no. He had to see for himself that the brave young woman with the fancy voice was okay.

With a final inward kick, he stepped into the room.

His eyes went straight to the bed. Fluffed up in white sheets, the little mama looked small and flushed. But good. Real good.

Her dark blond hair, sweaty and uncombed yesterday, was clean and neatly brushed and lay across her shoulders in a soft wave. She was prettier than he'd thought. Her thin face was blessed with long doe-shaped eyes the color of pancake syrup and a mouth that tipped up at the corners.

The thing that really drew his attention was the bundle nestled against her breast. A small egg-shaped head covered with a pink stocking cap protruded from a matching pink blanket. He could see the curve of the baby's cheek, the tiny button nose, the rise and fall of her body as she breathed. Thank God she was breathing smooth and even now.

He allowed himself to breathe, as well, aware that he hadn't quite believed the child would be alive.

The little mama saw the direction of his gaze and looked down at her baby with an expression that punched Dax in the gut. Mother love radiated from her. The kind Gavin had never known.

His admiration for the girl-woman, whatever she was, went up another notch. She loved her baby. She'd be a good mama.

He shifted, heard the scratchy sound of his boots against tile. What now? He'd seen what he came for. Could he just turn around and walk out?

"Would you like to see her?"

The words startled him, breaking through his thoughts of escape. Crushing the brim of his hat between tense fingers, he stepped closer to the bed and cleared the lump out of his throat. "She okay?"

"Perfect, thanks to you." The doe eyes looked up at him, again with that expression of trust.

"What about you?"

Roses bloomed on her cheeks. "Very well. Again thanks to you."

He'd embarrassed her, made her recall the liberties he'd taken with her body. He wanted to apologize, but he never seemed to know the right things to say to women.

"Would you like to hold her?" The little mama stretched the bundle in his direction. The blanket fell away from the baby's face and Dax went all mushy inside. He remembered how Gavin had looked those first few days. All squished and out of shape but so innocent Dax had fallen in instant, overpowering love.

Dax stepped away from the bed. "No."

He'd been to the feed store earlier. He couldn't be clean enough to hold a baby.

"Oh." The little mama's face fell. He felt like a jerk, but didn't figure it mattered. Once he was out of here, he'd never see her again.

"Sophie and I are grateful for everything you did."

"Sophie? Pretty."

"I thought so. Sophie Joy."

Feeling oversize, out of place and like a complete idiot, Dax nodded. "I gotta get back to the ranch. Just wanted to check on you."

"I appreciate it." She reached out a slender hand and touched his arm. Even through the long-sleeved jacket, Dax imagined the heat and pressure of her fingers seeping into his bloodstream. His mind went to the softness of the skin on her bare feet. She was probably silky all over.

Something inside him reacted like a wild

stallion. He jerked away. What the devil business did he have feeling attracted to a new mother, a woman young enough to be his…well, his niece or something. She was a kid. A kid. And he was a dirty old man.

Without another word, he spun away and hurried out the door, down the hall and out into the gray November where the Texas wind could slap some sense into him.

CHAPTER THREE

STUNNED, JENNA STARED as the cowboy retreated, turning his trim, anvil-shaped back toward her before charging out of the room as if a pack of dogs was after him.

"I don't think he likes us, Sophie," she murmured. Though she couldn't imagine why. He'd behaved the same way in the car yesterday, as though she'd angered him. Yet he'd helped her. And he'd come to visit her in the hospital.

"What a strange man."

He'd left so fast, the scent of a very masculine cologne lingered in the room like a contrail. Were all Texas cowboys so…reticent? Well, it didn't matter. She would likely never see the man again, and the truth was, Dax Coleman had saved her, saved Sophie, and she would be forever grateful.

Before she had time to ponder further, a woman entered the room. Dressed in a black pantsuit and white, round earbobs of the 1960s, the woman carried a clipboard and a stack of papers.

"I'm Alice Pernisky from the business office." She rolled an over-the-bed table in front of Jenna. "Let's put the baby in the bassinet while we take care of the paperwork."

Her no-nonsense style brooked no argument, so Jenna did as she said. She was worried enough about completing these forms.

"Let's take care of the birth certificate first." The woman pushed a paper under her nose. "The doctor has filled in the basics, but we'll need your complete information, your name, the father's name, and of course—" she allowed a thin smile "—the name you've chosen for your baby."

Heart thudding crazily, Jenna stared down at the form and wondered if falsifying a birth certificate was illegal. Ink pen hovering over the sheet, she considered long and hard.

After a few seconds, Alice Pernisky said, "My dear, if you don't want to put the father's name, that's fine. Just take care of the rest. We see more of that kind of thing than we used to."

Heat flushed from her toes to her head. They thought she was an unwed mother who had no idea who Sophie's father was.

"My husband died," she said, which was true, though Derek had been out of her life long before the car crash that killed him.

"I'm sorry," Alice said automatically, although Jenna did not think the woman believed her.

Would people always assume the worst if she didn't put Derek's name on the birth certificate?

Of course they would. This document would follow Sophie all the days of her life. And Jenna would not do that to her daughter.

Taking a deep breath, Jenna bent to the form and began to write. After the divorce, her parents had insisted she return to Carrington and she'd gladly done so. Derek had humiliated her enough. But now, his name might be the one thing that could keep her and Sophie from being discovered.

If she was going to start her life anew with Sophie, she would do it correctly. She would lie only if she had to, and pray her family wouldn't be able to trace her through hospital documents bearing only her married name.

As she handed over the form, another form appeared beneath. "Those are your release forms, your instructions on self-care, and of course your hospital bill. Do you have insurance we can file?"

Jenna gulped. Lie number one. "No."

"How do you plan to take of this? We take check or credit card, of course, and if need be, we can set up a payment plan."

"Cash. I'll pay cash."

The woman pulled back, startled. "Cash?"

"Yes." Accessing her bank accounts or using her credit cards would be too easy to trace. Until she and Sophie were established and on their own, she would not even consider such a thing. Maybe never. Cash was the only way.

Jenna reached for her handbag, aware of how out-of-place the designer crocodile looked in the hands of a woman without health insurance. As she withdrew the funds from her wallet, she had the absurd thought that Alice might think she'd stolen the bag, along with the money. What if she called the police?

Jenna's hand trembled as she counted out the correct amount and handed it over. She could feel the woman's curious stare and almost hear the wheels turning in her head.

When the last paper was signed and the woman left the room, Jenna felt light-headed with relief. Before putting her purse aside so she could hold Sophie again, she counted the remaining bills in her wallet. A quiver of worry drew her brows together. Never in her life had she needed to consider money. A Carrington simply grew up knowing there was plenty. Discussing personal finance was considered vulgar.

But she was no longer a Carrington. She was no longer one of Pennsylvania's old money debutantes with an endless supply of cash and credit cards. She was a single mother alone, scared… and nearly broke.

A tangle of nerves and hormones and uncertainty gathered inside Jenna a short time later as she leafed through two newspapers, including a national one, and waited to be dismissed from the hospital.

After careful scrutiny of each page, she sat back against the scratchy chair and let some of her tension ebb away. There was no mention of a missing heiress. At least, not yet.

She flipped to the classifieds of the local paper, the *Saddleback Sentinel,* and scanned the help wanted ads. After a couple of minutes, her lips curved in wry humor. If she could run a drilling rig or drive an eighteen-wheel truck, she'd be in business before nightfall.

"Looking for anything in particular?"

At Crystal's voice, Jenna jumped. The nurse stood in front of her with a wheelchair, smile curious.

The newspaper crinkled as Jenna refolded it and placed it on the nightstand. Part of her longed to confide in the friendly nurse and admit she needed a job. She opened her mouth to do just that but Sophie chose that moment to awake with a startled cry. All thought rushed to her baby.

"Is she all right?"

Crystal chuckled. "Yes, Jenna. She's fine. Baby's cry. Get used to it. Real used to it. I probably startled her with the noise of the wheelchair."

"Oh." Jenna fought down a blush and gingerly scooped her daughter from the Isolette. "Shh, darling, Mommy's here."

To her joy, Sophie stopped crying immediately. Her scrunched-up face relaxed as she blinked up at her mother. A swell of love ballooned in Jenna's chest.

"You two ladies ready for your free ride in a wheelchair?"

"Can't we walk?"

"Hospital regs, I'm afraid." Crystal patted the black seat. "Hop aboard the Wolf Express for the only free thing in this hospital."

With a smile at Crystal's humor, Jenna

complied, jittery to think that in a few minutes, she and Sophie would be alone and on their own. She'd known when she left the estate that this would happen, but she hadn't expected it to happen quite so soon. She'd hoped to be settled somewhere before Sophie's birth, to have the trunk full of layette items set up and ready for the baby's homecoming. She'd even had fantasies of a job where she could keep Sophie with her. Instead, she was down to her last few dollars with nowhere to take her newborn daughter.

Crystal guided the wheelchair down the long, pristine hospital corridor and out the exit toward the parking lot.

"So what did Dax have on his mind?"

The question startled Jenna. She'd tried to put the rugged cowboy out of her thoughts. "I'm not sure."

"What did he say?"

"He asked if Sophie and I were all right and then he left."

Crystal chuckled. "He's not a big talker."

"I noticed."

"Hunky, though, huh?"

"I suppose." She really didn't want to talk about the cowboy. "I think I scared him off."

"Nah. He's just quiet. I don't think anything scares Dax Coleman except his ex-wife."

"He's divorced?"

"Yep. For years, but as far as I know, he's never dated again. Reba did a number on him, the witch."

Jenna, in spite of herself, tilted her head in question. "Was she?"

Crystal hitched one shoulder. "I never liked her much, though some folks think the divorce was Dax's fault."

He wasn't exactly Mr. Congeniality, but after the way he'd helped her, she felt compelled to take his side. "Outsiders seldom know the full story."

She knew that from personal experience.

"Too true. And Dax has always been one of the good guys. Or he used to be."

Jenna let the subject of the cowboy drop. Something about him unsettled her in the oddest manner.

Wheels clattered over the concrete parking lot as Crystal pushed her and Sophie into the weak sunshine. The fresh air felt good on Jenna's skin after the stuffiness of the hospital.

Holding her pink-wrapped daughter snuggled close to her body, a few free baby supplies compliments of the hospital stuffed between her side and the arm of the chair, she couldn't help thinking how different this dismissal would have been in Philadelphia. Surrounded by masses of flowers, a private nurse, and at least two burly bodyguards—one for her and one for Sophie— she would have been gently hustled into a waiting car driven by Fredrick, the family chauffeur, and driven home to the nursery suite especially commissioned and furnished by her mother. There, in the stark white nursery, a nanny would have whisked Sophie from her arms and taken over every nuance of the baby's care. If Jenna was lucky and made enough fuss, she might get to hold her child occasionally.

No, she'd made the right decision, even if she had no idea where she would go or what she would do now.

The wheelchair slowed. "Which way is your car?"

"Out to the left, I think. It's a faded blue." She scanned the parking lot, hoping she'd recognize the still-unfamiliar vehicle. Was it only four days ago when, in an effort to conceal her true destination, she'd taken the train as far as Baltimore and purchased the car from a classified ad?

"There." She pointed, gripping Sophie tighter as Crystal picked up speed.

When they reached the car, the nurse held the baby while Jenna dug out her keys and unlocked the door.

"Someone washed my car," she said in wonder, gazing into the backseat. Someone had even cleaned the interior, which now smelled of vinyl cleaner instead of dust and designer perfume.

"Interesting," Crystal commented. "Must have been Dax."

"Why would he do that?"

The nurse shrugged. "Don't know, but it sure is interesting. Visiting you at the hospital and washing your car. Maybe he has a thing for new mothers."

Shocked, Jenna's snapped around to stare at the nurse. Crystal burst into laughter. "Girl, you should see your face. I was only teasing."

"Oh." But Jenna got that fluttery feeling in her stomach again. What was it about the mention of Dax Coleman that stirred her so?

"Where's your car safety seat?"

"My what?"

"Texas has a child safety seat law. You can't leave the hospital with Sophie until you have one installed."

One more thing she hadn't thought of. "Where can I get one?"

Crystal studied her from beneath black eyelashes. "The hospital sells them. If you'd like I'll run back inside and get one for you."

"Do you mind?"

"Not a bit." She named a price and Jenna extracted the required bills from her wallet.

"Cute purse," Crystal said. "Is that real alligator?"

"Crocodile. It was a gift," she hurried to say, downplaying her ability to purchase such a bag. What she really wanted to say was, "Want to buy it?" The cost of the handbag would go a long way toward apartment rent.

"Wish somebody would buy me gifts like that."

"No, you don't," she nearly said to the nurse's retreating back. You don't want someone to try to control you with money and things and fear.

While Crystal was gone, Jenna thought of her dwindling resources, spirits ebbing lower and lower. Even during her short marriage, they'd always had her considerable bank account, a fact that had changed her average Joe husband to Joe Millionaire in a matter of weeks.

She tasted the bitterness of his betrayal on her tongue. Before her name was dry on the marriage license, Derek, who had sworn he was not at all interested in Jenna's inheritance, had begun flashing her credit cards, living the high life and leaving her at home when she refused to play along.

"Here we go, Jenna." Crystal reappeared to pop open the back door and installed the car seat in short order. She held out her arms. "Give me the princess."

Jenna complied, happiness replacing the gloom. She wasn't alone anymore.

As the nurse settled the baby and strapped her in, Jenna watched, learning. She wasn't stupid. She was just inexperienced.

"All set." Crystal slammed the back door. Sophie's little arms jerked upward but before Jenna could rush to soothe her, she'd resettled.

"Thank you for everything, Crystal." Jenna slid behind the wheel, uncertainty overtaking her again. What now?

"You are as welcome as summer." Crystal, holding the driver's door open, leaned in, her dark eyes soft with concern. "Honey, are you going to be all by yourself with this new baby? Do you have anyone to help you?"

"Oh, certainly, I'll have plenty of—" Jenna lifted a hand to wave off the suggestion that she had no one and then let the hand fall against the warm steering column.

"No," she admitted, suddenly needing to talk to this young woman who was kindness personified. "My husband died. I'm alone, looking for a place to start fresh. I thought Sophie and I would be happier somewhere new, away from the memories." She gave a pathetic little laugh. "So here we are."

That much was absolutely true.

Crystal draped an arm over the top of the car door, all her weight on one hip. "So that explains it. I knew something was not right, but bless your heart, all alone. That's awful."

The woman's compassion was almost Jenna's undoing. She fought back a wave of self-pity, and then, angry at herself, she refused to acknowledge the emotion. She'd chosen this route even if things hadn't gone quite as smoothly as she'd planned. Starting fresh was the best thing for Sophie, no matter how difficult the first few weeks might be. She could do this. She wanted to do this. For her baby girl and even for herself. Alone was better than lonely and utterly dependent, with your life mapped out before you were out of diapers. Now that she had Sophie, she would never be lonely again.

Stiffening her spine, she said, "Can you direct me to a hotel?"

After a moment's consideration, Crystal took a scrap of paper from her uniform pocket and scribbled on it. "There's a little B and B over on Second Street, not fancy but decent and clean. Terri Wallace runs it. We graduated high school together. Nice gal. Tell her I sent you. I put my phone number on there, too. Call me if I can do anything. Or just to talk. I can always use a new friend."

A friend. Crystal couldn't begin to comprehend how much the offer heartened Jenna.

"Could I ask one more favor?"

"Name it."

"I need a job." She swallowed her pride and said the rest. "In a hurry. Do you have any suggestions?"

The darkly pretty face twisted in thought. "Can't think of anything right off."

Jenna's hopes fell. She pressed her lips together in dismay. Maybe Saddleback wasn't the right town. Maybe she should drive on to Austin or even on to Los Angeles, where she and Sophie could get lost in the masses. But she was too tired and shaky from childbirth to drive that far today.

"Listen," Crystal was saying. "The county employment office is located here in Saddleback. It might be worth a try." She rattled off an address. "In a few days, when you're feeling rested, just drive down Main Street. When you see the boot store—you can't miss it, there's an enormous sign out front shaped like a big red cowboy boot—the employment office is right across the street. Shirley McDougal runs the place. Sweet as pie. She knows everyone and everything in Saddleback. Go talk to her. Tell her I sent you."

"I don't know how I'll ever repay your generosity."

Crystal patted her shoulder. "Just take care of Princess Sophie and give me a call when you get settled. We'll have lunch or something."

Still stunned by the kindness of strangers in this Texas town, Jenna could only nod, fighting back the tears that suddenly clogged her throat.

Crystal stepped back from the car, lifting a hand to wave as Jenna slammed the door, cranked the engine and pulled out of the Saddleback Hospital parking lot.

CHAPTER FOUR

TEN DAYS LATER, Jenna knew she'd recuperated as long as her limited finances would allow. Twice during that time, Crystal Wolf had stopped by the B and B, spreading her brand of Texas hospitality, but Jenna had been afraid to tell her new friend just how desperate things were becoming.

After a sleepless night of baby care and worry, Jenna now stared at a pile of unfamiliar forms at the county employment agency while the woman named Shirley cooed and hummed to Sophie. From the moment she'd started the paperwork, Jenna had been stumped. About the only thing she could fill out easily was her name. She'd finally scribbled the address of the Red Rose Bed-and-Breakfast as her residence, but she had nothing to put in the experience and reference forms.

"What kind of work are you looking for, Jenna,

sugar?" Shirley asked, never looking up from Sophie's sleeping face.

"I'm not at all particular, but I would like to secure a position where I could keep my baby with me."

"Hmm. Well, that leaves out the fast-food places. I send a lot of folks to them. The junior high is always looking for substitutes, though you'd have to leave this precious one with a sitter." She glanced up, brows drawing together over her black plastic glasses. "Don't suppose you have a degree in education or computers?"

Jenna shook her head, hopes tumbling. "No."

She'd spent one semester at Brown University under the watchful eyes of her grandparents. Unfortunately, neither they nor her ever-present bodyguards were as watchful as her mother would have liked. She'd met Derek there. Heads had rolled but Mother's fury had come too late.

"How about the medical field? There's always a need for that. Nurses, paramedics, lab techs…"

Again Jenna shook her head. An overprotected heiress was a useless human being.

Shirley studied her beneath thick blond bangs. "Do you have any training? Any experience at all?"

Jenna's hopes fell even further as she bowed her head to the application and didn't answer. She could plan a dinner party for fifty, direct servants and organize a charity auction; none of those skills appeared all that useful in Saddleback, Texas.

Even if no one recognized her here, she might have to move on. Yet, Saddleback's friendliness and easy pace drew her. She wanted to remain in this remote place where her daughter had been born and where people treated her as just another person.

Shirley pushed her glasses up with one finger. "You don't seem the type, but would you mind doing domestic work? We get a few calls for that."

Domestics? As in a maid? Or a cook?

An idea popped into her head. She and Mother had taken a gourmet cooking class from a well-known chef. She'd loved it.

"Could I possibly keep Sophie with me?"

"That would be up to your employer, but I think most people would be all right with a little one around as long as you did the work."

"Then," Jenna said, suddenly thrilled at the idea, "I am a fabulous chef and quite amenable to domestics."

Surely, cleaning a house couldn't be that difficult. She'd watched the maids dozens of times.

Shirley grinned. "My dear girl, I think I may have something for you. A family outside of town needs a cook and general housekeeper. Want to check it out?"

A renewed zip of energy had Jenna sitting up straighter. "Absolutely."

The woman returned a still-sleeping Sophie to Jenna's arms and then riffled through a set of files, pulling out a card.

"Here you go," she said, handing the information to Jenna. "I'll call and let him know you're coming for an interview."

Jenna was beyond delighted, though admittedly a bit nervous as she gripped the index card in her fingers. This was her opportunity to start life all over again, to make a life for herself and Sophie, to finally be her own person.

With held breath, she glanced at the name and address of her prospective employer.

The information she read froze the smile on her lips.

Southpaw Cattle Company. Dax Coleman.

Dax slammed the telephone receiver down, then looked around the living room to be sure no one was listening before letting out a curse.

Last night, he'd dreamed of the little mama and her baby. Again. Then he'd lain awake, staring up at the dark ceiling as he listened to a north wind rattle the trees outside and wondered if the fragile pair was all right.

They haunted him. He couldn't get them out of his head, a fact that infuriated him.

Now a phone call to the hospital told him exactly nothing. What had he expected? The day he'd visited her, he hadn't even thought to ask her name. He'd just asked for the mother and baby he'd brought into the emergency room. How stupid was that? All the receptionist would tell him was that mother and baby had been discharged, but unless Dax was next of kin, and she knew danged well he wasn't, no other information could be shared.

A distant relative of Reba's, the hateful old biddy had never liked him anyway. She'd enjoyed putting him in his place.

"Fine," he said to absolutely no one. The little mama and her baby were gone. They were all right. He could forget them. They were not his responsibility. He had enough of that to choke a horse already. End of topic.

No use fretting over a baby girl he'd never see again when he had his own problems to contend with. Shirley down at the employment office was sending him a new recruit this morning.

He laughed, a mocking sound. Good old Shirley had warned him she was sick and tired of finding him housekeepers only to have him run them off with his cranky-butted attitude. Her words. Cranky-butted. He could almost see her shaking her finger in his face.

He'd laughed when she'd said it. Now he wondered. Was he cranky-butted? Was he a bitter man with a bad attitude? Was that why Reba had walked out, leaving behind a new baby, a husband who'd adored her and an easy life?

He kicked a chair leg. Reba and her betrayal was not allowed in this house.

Dax snatched up the two empty glasses and a corn dog wrapper from the coffee table, toting them to the big, silver, step-levered trash can in the kitchen. Silly to feel nervous about interviewing a prospective housekeeper, but he needed to get this woman on board right away. Rushing home to meet Gavin's school bus each evening took a bite out of his productivity.

He trailed back through the living room, wiping a shirtsleeve over the fireplace mantel then grimaced to discover his shirt was now covered in dust. He batted at it and sneezed when the dust flew upward, dancing in the overhead light.

The doorbell chimed.

As he strode across the carpet toward the foyer, he noticed two of Gavin's miniature cars and a sock sticking out from under the couch—along with a dust bunny the size of a jack rabbit.

He gave up. He was a rancher. This was why he hired housekeepers.

With a final slap at his dusty shirtsleeve Dax yanked the front door open. His mouth also fell open as he looked down into a familiar face. A very young, slender and decidedly pretty face.

Blast it.

What the devil was the little mama doing on his porch? Please, please. Surely not to apply for the housekeeper position.

Hot on the heels of his plea was a thrill that rocked him to his boot tips. Double blast and a dozen other curses. A burned-out old cowboy like him getting palpitations over a teenager.

"Mr. Coleman?"

Given his wayward thought processes and after what they'd shared in her car, hearing her refer to him as Mr. Coleman was creepy. He should call the sheriff on himself.

"Dax," he growled, wondering why he was in such a weird mood. His gaze went to the pink bundle in her arms and stayed there. "How's the little one?"

"Wonderful. Perfect."

"Good."

They seemed destined to repeat the same sentences to each other. Blast it.

Finding his manners, though admittedly a bit rusty, he stepped aside and motioned toward the interior. "Want to come in?"

She came inside, moving past him with a grace and elegance that had him thinking of ballerinas and her pretty feet again. He caught a whiff of that flowery perfume he'd smelled in her car. As if his eyelids ruled his body, they dropped closed and he inhaled. Nice. Really nice.

"Dax?"

His eyelids flew open. Why had he invited her inside?

"Have a seat," he said, feeling about as awkward as a three-legged horse.

He peered out the door, craning his neck to look down the long, long driveway. Nothing but her blue car. Where was the real housekeeper? Please let her pull up soon.

"Are you expecting someone?" the little mama asked, still standing in the middle of his foyer and close enough for him to see the flecks of gold in her eyes.

He backed up a step.

"A housekeeper applicant from the employment office is on her way out."

The little mama turned bright pink. "Oh," she said. "That would be me."

She handed him a card bearing the logo of the county employment office and her name, Jenna Garwood. Dax's heart stopped. Jenna Garwood was the name Shirley had given him. Oh no.

"You?"

Her pink drained away. "Is there a problem? I can cook. I'm an accomplished chef."

Dax was already shaking his head. "I don't think so."

The last thing he wanted was this new mama who haunted his dreams to live here. She was probably a teenage runaway. He'd get arrested just for thinking about the way her eyebrows took wing at the ends and for noticing how full and pouty her lips were. She was trouble with a baby in arms.

"I need a mature woman to look after my boy."

"I can do that."

"This ranch is far from town. It gets lonely out here."

"I'm accustomed to solitude."

Getting desperate now, Dax pointed to the infant. "You have a new baby."

"I promise to keep up with my domestic duties and care for her, as well. Mothers have maintained homes for millennia while rearing children." Her doe-eyes had widened, almost pleading. "I can do it."

Before he did something really stupid, Dax grumbled, "No."

The little mama—Jenna Garwood—drew up to her full height, which wasn't much, come to think of it. "May I inquire as to why?"

Inquire as to why? What kind of question was that? Finally, he blurted, "How old are you?"

The corners of her too-full lips tilted up. "I'm twenty-two. Why? Age has nothing to do with anything."

Oh, yes it did. He was thirty-four years old and she wasn't.

"A young girl like you—" he started.

"I'm not a girl. I'm a woman—with a baby to support."

Like he didn't know that.

"I know this isn't ideal. Not for me, either, but I really need this job, Mr. Coleman."

"Dax," he growled. And what did she mean, this

wasn't ideal for her, either? What was wrong with his ranch? "I have a son. He's in kindergarten."

"I have a daughter. You delivered her."

Jenna Garwood did not play fair. Had she intuitively known he felt some kind of warped sense of responsibility for her and the baby?

The baby in her arms squeaked, squirming. Dax felt a momentary reprieve from this miserable conversation. "She's awake."

That motherly Madonna sweetness moved across Jenna Garwood's face. "Will you hold her for a minute while I get the diaper bag from the car? She's probably wet."

Dax swallowed hard and made no move to take the offered baby.

"She won't bite." That precise, clipped voice chided him for being a coward.

Him? A coward? "Get the bag."

As if he was hypnotized, he reached out, awkward at first as he took the tiny bundle in his arms.

Jenna wasted no time heading for her car.

The front door snapped shut. The baby startled in that special way only newborns do. With fingers too big and thick to be handling an infant again, Dax peeled back the blanket and looked down into a face as pink and new as a rosebud.

His heart did a funny jitterbug in his chest. He remembered when Gavin was this small and helpless. He remembered how scared and alone he'd felt knowing he was the only parent with sole responsibility for another human being.

Did Jenna Garwood feel that way, too? There was dignity in her voice but a look of desperation in her eyes that he understood too well.

The baby mewed and made that squeaky, about-to-cry sound. Tiny, gossamer eyelids lifted. A pair of dark blue eyes snagged him as if he were a marlin and she were a giant hook.

With an inner groan, he knew he was in trouble. Big trouble.

He'd been in Jenna Garwood's shoes. He'd been alone with a newborn—alone and desperate.

And, though he was sure he'd live to regret his rash, emotional decision, he was going to hire her.

CHAPTER FIVE

JENNA MOVED IN that afternoon.

She had plenty of reservations about living on the remote ranch with a man she barely knew, but she and Sophie were out of choices. She was troubled that Dax Coleman hadn't wanted to hire her at first and then had suddenly changed his mind. Troubled and curious.

For those few minutes when she'd gone to the car for Sophie's diapers, she'd been certain he would send her away. She'd returned to the house prepared to beg and lie and make up references, only to discover that his attitude had completely reversed.

The perplexing rancher had been sitting in a leather rocking chair with Sophie cradled against his chest. For one moment, Jenna had remained in the foyer watching and aching with the knowledge that Sophie would not have a father to cradle her. She'd listened as Dax murmured softly to the baby in a way that turned Jenna's insides to warm honey. When she'd made her presence known, he'd gone silent.

But she'd heard. And that moment had told her a great deal about Dax Coleman.

By the time she had driven to the B and B for her belongings, then returned to the ranch, Dax was nowhere to be seen. A slim, nice-looking cowboy who appeared amused with the world greeted her at the front door.

"Well, ain't you a pretty little thing?" His grin widened as his gaze slid over her. "Old Dax must be going blind."

Jenna blinked, startled and uncomfortable. What exactly did he mean? That Dax thought she was ugly? Not that it mattered one iota what Dax thought about her appearance. She had no illusions about her looks, but still, a woman didn't like thinking her appearance was the topic of dinner conversation.

A dry leaf swirled from beneath a fat oak tree in the yard and glided around her head. The weather today was colder and she was eager to get Sophie inside.

"I'm Jenna Garwood, the new housekeeper."

The admission sounded strange on her lips. She was some-one's housekeeper.

The ranch hand crossed a pair of muscled arms over his chest. "You sure are. I'm Rowdy Davis, Dax's ranch manager. He said you'd be coming back soon."

No wonder the man was behaving in such an insolent manner. His boss—and hers—wasn't here. For very realistic reasons, she trusted the rancher who'd rescued her and had expected him to be here. Rowdy Davis, on the other hand, made her nervous.

Clutching Sophie closer, she glanced around, suddenly feeling alone and vulnerable. All she saw was barns and fences and acres and acres of serenely grazing cattle. In the distance several cowboys rode horses across a field. They were so far away no sound carried on the wind except the occasional bawl of a calf.

Jenna licked dry lips. It wasn't every day a Carrington hired on as a domestic and encountered a leering cowboy. The man must be either out of his head with loneliness or the kind of guy who thought every female was fair game. Jenna suspected the latter. But she was a new mother with a baby in arms that grew heavier with every second. The opposite sex was the last thing on her mind.

"Where is Mr. Coleman?"

The cowboy got that look again as if he was holding back a laugh. "Gavin got a bloody nose on the playground so Dax went to pick him up."

"Gavin?"

"Dax's son."

Gavin. Of course. He'd mentioned a son.

"Come on in. I'm supposed to help you with your things."

The man pushed the door open and stepped to one side. Finally, he was demonstrating some knowledge of etiquette. Miss Manners would have been aghast at his previous behavior.

Holding Sophie's diaper bag against her side with one elbow, she started into the warm foyer. The cowboy's body crowded the narrow space. Jenna slanted slightly to one side, hoping he'd get the message that with her load, and attired in a heavy woolen coat, she needed more room. He didn't budge. He didn't even offer to help. Her backside accidentally brushed against him. She jerked away, face hot, and moved across the stone-tiled entry to the carpeted area beyond.

When she glanced back, Rowdy remained in the doorway, grinning. Her flush deepened.

"I have a number of things in the car if you

wouldn't mind getting them please," she said stiffly, hearing the haughty tone her mother reserved for servants. Hopefully, the man would get the message that she did not want to play his game—whatever it was.

Rowdy's dark eyes glittered and continued staring at her several beats longer before he said, "I'll get them in a minute. Let's get you and baby situated first."

Jenna felt flustered. She wasn't sure what to make of Rowdy Davis. He had done nothing wrong, but he looked at her in a way that was disconcerting, as though he knew her secrets, as though he knew something she didn't.

He was young and good-looking and a tad bit cocky. Maybe that was her problem. His confidence was the antithesis of hers.

The sooner he went on his way, the sooner she could relax.

"Would you mind showing me to my quarters?" she asked. "Then I won't trouble you any longer."

The corner of Rowdy's mouth hiked higher. "Sure thing, ma'am. Your *quarters* are this way." He emphasized the word. "And you aren't troubling me one little bit."

"Thank you," she said, mustering her dignity. "I should like to see them."

Still wearing a strange smirk, Rowdy led the way down a hallway to the left of the massive living/dining area. He ambled in front of her with a slow swagger as if wanting her to notice his lean, fit body and tight blue jeans. Purposefully, she focused her attention elsewhere.

The ranch home was lovely in a Western manner. Spacious and well-appointed in colors and textures that glowed with warmth and re-flected light from a pair of large patio doors in the dining area. The ranch was so different from the old mansion she'd escaped, and its modern warmth drew her like a magnet. She could really enjoy tending to such a lovely place.

"Dax wants you to have this section of rooms," Rowdy was saying as he pushed open a door down a hall and to the back of the kitchen area. "This larger bedroom has an adjoining bath and opens into a smaller room intended as a nursery."

"Oh, this should do nicely. Thank you."

Rowdy chuckled again as if she'd said some-thing amusing. She didn't understand his behavior. But then her experience with the opposite sex was limited to one cheating husband, her absentee father and a host of older male employees.

"Dax set up the crib already. Said you could arrange things any way you wanted."

Jenna stopped in the doorway and lowered the diaper bag to the floor. Still unaccustomed to the weight of a baby and a bag, her arm ached. "He bought a crib for Sophie?"

"Gavin's old crib was in storage. Dax just dragged it out of the shed and cleaned it up a little."

The kindness created a warm glow in her chest. After purchasing the blue car, she'd used her credit cards for the final time at a baby store. Then she'd stuffed as many items as possible for Jenna's care into the trunk and headed west. The layette included a folding travel bed—the best she could do in a small car—but a real crib was even better.

"I shall have to thank him."

Rowdy grinned. "Indeed, you shall."

A flush of embarrassment rushed up her neck. Enough was enough. "Mr. Davis, are you making fun of me?"

"We call it teasing around these parts."

"May I inquire as to the reason?"

"You talk funny. All citified and stiff. Kinda tickles the ears."

"Oh, I see." Was her speech the only thing he found amusing? Had she been imagining his insolent stares?

She moved deeper into the room, eager to settle Sophie and to explore her new living arrangements. Rowdy remained in the doorway watching her. "Thank you for showing me the rooms. I'm sure I can find my way around from here."

The ranch hand didn't seem to get the message. He slouched against the door facing, picking at the button on his sleeve.

Determined not to let him bother her, Jenna lifted Sophie to her shoulder and turned her attention to the room.

The suite was different than the rest of the wood and stone and leather ranch house. Here was an English garden, a room filled with lush, print fabrics and graceful furnishings in sage and antique white with splashes of rose and blue. The decor bled over into a sitting room and through to the nursery. Jenna loved it.

"This looks new. As though no one has ever used it," she murmured.

"I don't think it was used much."

Sophie made one of her squeaky noises and

squirmed. Jenna patted the tiny back as she turned toward Rowdy. "But these rooms are the nursery. Didn't Gavin sleep here?"

"That was before my time, but I doubt it."

"Why ever not? The rooms are beautiful."

He shrugged. "I guess beauty's in the eye of the beholder."

His answer was no answer at all, but Jenna didn't press the topic. If Dax didn't like the look of an English garden, why should she care? Her job was to cook and clean, not question the tastes of her employer.

A little thrill ran through her veins. She had acquired a job and she would be able to care for her daughter. Like a normal person.

Grateful, she left Rowdy Davis standing in the door while she took Sophie into the taupe-walled nursery and laid her in the crib. As she placed a kiss on her daughter's velvet cheek, the soft scent of baby breath and formula filled her senses. She thought the smell was pure heaven.

She slipped out of her coat and draped it over the railing.

Someone, Dax she supposed, had neatly made up the baby bed and placed pretty quilted bumper pads around the inside. A quilt rack complete with a darling patchwork quilt in sage and taupe stood next to the bed.

Jenna adjusted her daughter's blanket and stroked the miniscule hand, lost in a love that brought a lump to her throat. Sophie looked tiny in the big crib.

"I was just wondering something."

Jenna jumped at the sudden intrusion of a man's voice. She hadn't realized Rowdy had followed her through to the nursery.

She turned slightly to find him standing at her elbow. "Yes? What is it?"

"What's a pretty girl like you doing out here?" He edged closer, overpowering her nose with his heavy-handed cologne. "I can't believe any man would let something like you get away. You married?"

The question startled her like an unexpected spray of cold water.

"I'm a widow. Sophie's father died in a car crash."

"My sympathies." The words didn't quite match the expression in his eyes.

"Thank you." She swallowed and slanted away to fuss with the elephant mobile hanging above Sophie. She expected Rowdy to take his leave.

He didn't. Instead, he reached into the crib and

drew a fingertip over Sophie's rose-petal cheek. Jenna had to restrain herself to keep from pushing his hand away.

"So you and the little darlin' here are all alone in the world?" He straightened, turning his probing gaze to her.

"We are making our own way quite well, thank you."

"Good for you. But if you should need a man, give a holler." His words were soft, suggesting something more than helping her unload her car. "I'm always glad to help out."

Jenna had no idea how to handle the man. Pretending a fascination with the little lamp atop the armoire, she moved in that direction. She could feel Rowdy's stare on her back. Maybe he was just being friendly, but his sly, unyielding grin made her uncomfortable as if he could see through her clothes.

Surreptitiously, she glanced down to check her buttons. Though her breasts were uncomfortably full and pushed against her smocked top, she was covered and decent.

"Rowdy!" A gravelly voice called from the front of the house.

Jenna turned toward the sound, a sense of relief

flooding her. She was probably being silly but Dax's gruff voice was a welcome sound.

"Back here, boss." Rowdy aimed a wink in her direction and stepped to the doorway. "I'm showing the lady her quarters."

"Her what?" Dax appeared behind Rowdy, a scowl on his face.

"She talks prissified. Called her room *quarters,* like this was the Taj Mahal or something. Pretty little thing, though," he said as if she wasn't standing right there.

Dax's scowl deepened. "Where's her stuff? I told you to help her."

Rowdy pushed off the doorway, seemingly undisturbed by Dax's bluster. "I was just about to get it out of the car."

"Go on then. I'll help you in a minute."

"No problem. I can handle it." With a final flicker in her direction, Rowdy strode out of the room.

Dax's gaze followed him for a minute before he turned his attentions to Jenna. "Everything all right? You getting settled?"

Other than not liking his ranch hand, she was delighted.

"I haven't been here long enough to get settled, but your home is lovely." Although it needed a thorough dusting. "The English garden decor in here is wonderful."

"English garden?" Bewildered green eyes blinked around the room. "Is that what you call this stuff?"

His clueless response made her want to laugh. In his black cowboy hat, sheepskin jacket and a pair of scuffed boots, he didn't exactly fit the image of a man who would be comfortable in an English garden or a room filled with soft colors and ruffles and baby things. Perhaps a nanny had occupied this suite.

"Thank you for thinking of the crib."

"Might as well get some use out of it. Baby need anything else?"

Dax stepped to the crib and gazed down. His shoulders relaxed as though looking at Sophie melted the tension from him. When he reached down and placed his wide hand lightly on the baby's chest, something warm and tender moved inside of Jenna.

The notion puzzled her. She hadn't wanted Rowdy to touch her baby, but she felt differently with Dax. Maybe because those rough rancher hands had brought Sophie safely into the world.

"She breathes so softly," she said, moving to his side, intuitively understanding his reason for touching the newborn. Hadn't she done the same thing dozens of times over the past few days?

Dax turned his head, bringing his face close to hers. "Like a whisper."

Jenna stared into those green, green eyes, the funny, unsettled stirring coming back in full force. Dax made her uncomfortable, too, but in a far different way than she felt with Rowdy. He was short-spoken and puzzling, but she would trust him with her life. A tiny smile quivered on her lips. Indeed, she had already done that.

Dax looked at her for another long, curious moment before moving to the window. He pushed aside the taupe draperies and looked out. "Wonder what's keeping Rowdy?"

Footsteps thudded down the hall. "That must be him."

"Slow as Christmas," Dax grumbled, relieving his ranch hand of a giant carton and a suitcase.

"You wouldn't believe all the junk she crowded into that trunk. Women and their stuff."

Dax made a harrumphing noise in the back of his throat. "Typical."

Jenna wasn't sure what he meant, but from his darkened expression she decided not to ask. She did, however, want to ask about the little boy.

As soon as Rowdy disappeared for another load, she did.

"Rowdy said your son had a bloody nose. Where is he? Did you take him to the hospital?"

Dax made a face as though the notion was ridiculous. "He's all right. I sent him to wash his hands."

A small boy poked his head around the corner. Except for a pair of cobalt-blue eyes, he was a miniature version of his father. "I falled off the merry-go-round. My shirt's all bloody."

"I told you to change clothes."

Gavin's face puckered. "I forgot."

The child looked so small and worried, Jenna crouched in front of him. "I'm Jenna. I'm going to be your new chef."

"I'm Gavin Matthew Coleman."

"A handsome name for a handsome boy. From all that blood on your shirt, I'd say you must be a brave boy, too."

"Noah said I was going to die. He's my friend. I was kinda scart."

Dax made an impatient noise. "No one dies of a bloody nose."

Jenna ignored the irritation in Dax's voice as she tilted the child's chin. Dried blood ringed his nostrils. "I think we need to wash your face a bit, too, and perhaps have a nice warm bath and change that shirt."

"We were about to do that," Dax said. "Go on, Gavin. I'll be there directly."

The boy lingered in front of Jenna. "Are you the new cooker?"

Jenna smiled. Obviously, Gavin was unfamiliar with the term chef. "I am indeed."

The child gave an exaggerated sigh. "What a relief."

Behind her Dax snorted. "Tired of pizza, sport?"

Jenna patted the boy's narrow shoulder. "I shall prepare a dinner fit for two kings. Now head for that bath. Kings must be well-groomed."

"You talk funny, but I like you," Gavin said and surprised her with a quick hug before darting out of the room.

"That's a first."

She stood, turning to look at the rancher. He wore a bemused expression. "What is?"

"Gavin is bashful. I've never seen him hug a housekeeper before."

"Then, I shall take that as a great compliment. He's a darling boy."

"And about that meal fit for two kings?"

"Yes?"

"It might have to wait until you go grocery shopping."

When she laughed, Dax Coleman did a strange thing. He slapped his Stetson on his head, turned on his boot heel and stalked out.

CHAPTER SIX

DAX STOMPED HIS BOOTS at the back door and watched clumps of dirt and unmentionable debris fall away. He should have stayed in the house and made sure the new housekeeper did all right with Gavin. Rowdy could have seen to the cow with the bad foot.

Might as well face the truth, Coleman. The new housekeeper with her big innocent eyes and sexy laugh scared you off.

Jenna Garwood stirred feelings in him that he'd killed long ago. And he didn't like it. Especially from her, a slip of a girl far too young for him to be noticing. Now she was going to be in his house and under his nose, smelling like flowers all the time.

What had he been thinking?

What kind of father was he that he'd leave his son alone with a stranger? He hadn't even asked for references this morning, which showed just how stupid he was. He might have hired Jane the Ripper.

Yet, he wasn't worried about his son in Jenna's care. Not in the least. He'd watched from the doorway while she had filled the bathtub and tested the water with her delicate fingers. She'd told the boy he was brave and strong as Gavin related the bloody nose incident in a child's convoluted manner. And she'd promised to read him a bedtime story.

None of those things kept her from being a serial killer, but Dax simply knew his son was safe with the new mother. Now, it was Dax's job to make sure the new mother was safe from her employer.

As he pushed open the back door, the scent of cooking wafted from the kitchen. He had no idea what the new housekeeper had found to cook in those cereal- and macaroni-laden cupboards, but it sure smelled good.

He chuckled. Anything smelled good to a man who'd been eating his own very bad cooking.

As he entered the kitchen, Jenna shot him a tentative smile. She'd found an apron somewhere and pulled her hair back into a hair clip. She looked about sixteen.

That's the way he needed to think about her.

She looked sixteen. A kid. He had never lusted after teenagers.

His traitorous brain registered ample womanly breasts and curvy hips. Her new-mother's body looked far older than sixteen.

Blast his eyes for noticing.

"Dinner in five minutes," she said.

He wanted to tell her the food smelled good and he was starving. Instead, he grumbled, "Where's Gavin?"

She pointed an oversize wooden spoon toward the living room. "Diligently practicing the letter *A*. *A* is for *apple* and *ant* and *aaa-choo,* you know."

Again that smile that gave him belly flips.

"Gavin," he hollered. "Come on. Wash up."

His son appeared, toting a pencil and a piece of wide-lined paper. "I finished my *A*."

Dax took the page in hand to admire the squiggly effort. "Looks good, sport."

The smell of flowers and bacon assailed him as Jenna peered over his shoulder. "Lovely job, Gavin. Your teacher will be very impressed."

Gavin beamed up at Jenna as if she'd given him a year's supply of ice cream. Any fool could see the little dude craved a woman's praise. Blast Reba for her abandonment. Leaving her husband was one thing. Abandoning her son was inexcusable.

"Put your work away and wash your hands for supper," he told the boy.

"I took a bath already," Gavin said as he stuffed the paper down into his schoolbag.

"Doesn't matter." Dax led the way to the back of the house with Gavin dragging his feet behind. By the time they returned to the dining room, the long oak table had been transformed.

The new housekeeper, or chef as she liked to say, apparently had discovered the fancy dishes Reba had purchased and never used—dishes he'd never bothered to use, either. Two places were set with matching plates and silverware, along with dark green cloth napkins and gleaming stemware. A candlestick graced each end of the table—who knew where she'd found those?—and in the center was a slender vase poked full of backyard weeds arranged in artsy beauty.

"What's all this? A party?"

Jenna blinked in surprise. "No, sir. Dinner."

"Never seen such a fancy table for a mere meal." For a bachelor and his child who often ate in front of the television or at the bar, this was like dining at the Ritz.

"Shall I serve now?" she asked, hovering as if worried about pleasing him. The notion made him mad. All he expected was a meal, not subservience.

"Just put the food on the table." He scraped out a chair for Gavin and then for himself. "We aren't helpless."

Face flushed, she did as he said, sliding a steaming casserole in front of him. "You were right about the cupboards being bare. I'll have to rectify that tomorrow."

He eyed the dish with suspicion. "What is this?"

"A macaroni-and-cheese quiche."

"I like macaroni," Gavin said. A doubtful Dax scooped a helping onto both of their plates. Wasn't there some kind of rule that men didn't eat quiche? What *was* quiche anyway?

"And," Jenna went on, standing so close he could still smell perfume, "baked potato soup with herbed toast points."

Toast points? He eyed the toasted triangles arranged in a tidy circle on a serving plate. Some kind of green leaf adorned the center.

He had to hand it to the new cook, the food was pretty. Might as well find out if it was edible.

"Dig in, Gavin." He could have saved his breath because the boy had already shoveled macaroni into his mouth until he resembled a chipmunk. "Slow down, boy."

"It's good, Daddy." Though muffled, the words matched the pleasure on Gavin's face.

Dax took a bite. His taste buds shouted for joy. Whatever quiche was, it included bacon and to his way of thinking, anything with bacon was good.

"Could I get anything else for you?" Jenna asked.

She looked tired. Dax wanted to kick himself. She was a new mama, not much more than a week away from having a baby. She shouldn't be slaving over a stove.

"Sit down," he said.

"Is everything all right with the food?" She drew her pouty bottom lip between her teeth.

Dax frowned. He needed no reminders that she had a mouth made for kissing. "Sit down. Eat."

"I'm the chef, not a guest."

"I'm the boss. Sit. Eat."

Gavin's head volleyed back and forth between the adults, expression worried.

Jenna hovered between the kitchen island and the dining table, looking as anxious as Gavin did. The notion that both of them were getting nervous made Dax feel like a jerk.

"Sit," he bellowed.

Jenna dropped an apple-red pot holder and slithered into the farthest chair from him.

"There is no need to shout," she said with a dignity that turned his annoyance to amusement. Posture stiff and nostrils flared, Jenna Garwood had gone from scared chick to mad hen faster than a mosquito bite.

Dax scooted back from the table and rose. "You need a plate."

She started up. "I'll get it."

"Sit," he said again, this time in a gentler voice. "You've done enough."

He retrieved the plate and utensils and put them in front of her. She looked flustered and pink and tired.

He kicked himself again.

"You've overdone it," he said, taking up his fork. "I shouldn't have let you start tonight."

She flashed him a puzzled look.

"I'm perfectly well, thank you." With graceful fingers she filled her plate and began to eat.

"How's the baby?" He shoved a bite of something cheesy into his mouth and chewed.

Jenna delicately patted her lips with a green napkin. "She sleeps most of the time."

"Don't worry. It won't last. How often does she

wake in the night?" He couldn't believe he was having this conversation.

"Twice so far. Nights are the hardest." She dipped a spoon into the steaming soup and stirred. "I'm having difficulty forcing myself to think clearly when I'm half-asleep."

"Yes. I remember the feeling."

"You do?" Her gaze flicked to Gavin, who continued stuffing macaroni into his face as if he hadn't eaten in weeks. It occurred to Dax that he'd neglected teaching his son some common manners.

He tapped Gavin's forearm. "Slow down, sport. There's plenty."

Gavin grinned. Soup dripped on his chin. Before Dax could reprimand him, Jenna handed the boy a napkin and silently indicated the drip. When Gavin successfully swiped the spot, she reacted as though he'd conquered Mt. Everest. "Splendid, Gavin." She clapped her hands once beneath her chin. "I can see your handsome face so much better."

Gavin beamed a hundred-watt grin. "You make good soup."

"Thank you. A chef appreciates hearty appetites." She tasted the soup, her gaze observing Dax above the spoon. "Did you get up with Gavin when he was a baby?"

He hadn't intended to go there. "Yeah."

Her unspoken question hovered like a housefly, annoying him. Where was Gavin's mother? Why hadn't she cared for her son? Well, he wasn't going to talk about Reba, especially in front of Gavin. The boy had enough questions without stirring up more.

"I think that's an admirable thing," Jenna said.

Dax scowled. He'd missed something. "What is?"

"For a father to dedicate himself to the care of an infant." She tilted her head toward Gavin. "You must have been a very special baby."

Gavin looked pleased. "Did your daddy take care of you, too?"

Something tightened in her face. He was certain Gavin wouldn't notice but Dax had. That she was bothered by the question gave rise to new concerns about the woman he'd hired to care for his son. Who was Jenna Garwood anyway?

"No, I lived in the city," she said a little too brightly before glancing down at her plate. Dax wondered what living in the city had to do with Gavin's question about her father.

When she looked up again, her smile was as fake as Reba's fingernails. "You are such a lucky boy. You live on a wonderful ranch with your dad and all these animals. Can you ride a horse?"

Gavin dropped his head and fiddled with a piece of toast. "Not yet."

"Horses scare him." The notion perturbed Dax no end, but he was trying to be patient. Everything scared Gavin. Horses, cows, loud noises, hoot owls. The boy jumped at shadows.

The new housekeeper was all sympathy. "How old are you Gavin?"

"Five. I'll be six February 17."

She waved a hand. "You have plenty of time to learn equestrian skills."

Gavin's fork paused over the cheesy casserole. "Huh?"

"Riding a horse," Dax said. Rowdy was right. She did talk funny. She was far too refined to be a housekeeper. "Equestrian refers to horses."

"Oh." The word was too much for the boy so he let it slide. "When I get big I'll ride. Daddy will get me an old broke pony when I'm ready. All I have to do is the say the word. Right, Daddy?"

Dax's mouth twisted. He'd said that very thing to Gavin a dozen times. "Right, sport."

"And you will become a wonderful horseman, I am certain." Jenna favored Gavin with a smile

and reached for another toast point. *Toast points.*
He was still tickled over that one.

While the heavy dose of over-the-top kindness
floated around his kitchen table, Dax's brain was
also shooting off all kinds of warning signals.
Jenna Garwood had come into his life in a bizarre
manner and, like her pretty little toast points, she
no more fit on a ranch than he fit at that pink hotel
in Hollywood.

Clearing his throat, Dax interrupted the pleasant
chit-chat. "Where you from, Jenna? I forgot to
ask this morning during our interview."

Some interview. She'd handed him that soft
little baby, looked at him with worried eyes, and
he'd forgotten to use the good sense his mama
had given him.

"I beg your pardon?" she asked, dragging her
attention away from his son.

"Your application was a little short on details.
I was asking where you're from."

"Oh." She had that deer-in-the-headlights look.
Her hands fidgeted with the napkin. "I'm from
back East." She hopped up from the table. "Let me
clear away the plates and bring dessert."

Gavin whooped for joy. "Dessert! She made
dessert, Daddy."

Jenna disappeared around the bar and into the kitchen. Dax shoved back from the table and stalked after her. She was going to talk to him and she was going to do it now. All the dessert in the world wasn't stopping him from finding out more about her.

Her back was turned when he entered the kitchen area. Busy dishing up something onto his fancy saucers, she pretended not to hear his approach. Incensed, he moved closer. When she still didn't turn around, he slammed a hand down on each side of her. She couldn't run now. He'd trapped her.

Leaning next to her ear, he growled, "Are you trying to avoid my questions?"

With a gasp, Jenna whirled around, eyes wide as those saucers. "What do you mean?"

Cripes. She was so near he could feel her body heat. And smell that tantalizing perfume. What had he been thinking to move in this close?

Sweat popped out on the back of his neck. He dug his fingers into the countertop and hung on tight. Regardless of the unwanted physical reaction to his new employee, he deserved answers.

"I need to know more about you than the fact that you cook weird food."

If such a thing was possible, she drew farther back, pressing into the counter behind her.

"Weird?" Her eyes widened some more, this time in dismay. Her pouty mouth turned down. "You didn't like it?"

Blast and be danged. He'd hurt her feelings. He tried again. "I didn't mean weird. Different."

"Different?" She still didn't look happy. And her too-near chest rose and fell as if she might cry.

"Different but good," he said, growing more unraveled by the moment. A smart man would back away from her lush body and her sweet eyes and her tantalizing mouth. A smart man would never have come in here in the first place. "Real good. You're a great cook."

She was beginning to brighten. He wanted her to smile again the way she'd been smiling at Gavin all through supper... Dinner... Whatever she wanted to call it. "I haven't eaten such a meal in weeks."

Actually, he'd never eaten such a meal, but he knew when to cut his losses and keep his mouth shut.

She relented a little and Dax thought he saw a hint of humor lurking in those eyes. Brown eyes. Like the color of honey. Sweet, warm, delectable honey.

Why didn't someone just shoot him now?

"I'm glad," she murmured, the softness of her breath brushing his lips. Temptation tortured him. If he leaned in the slightest bit, they'd be touching from chest to thigh. A little closer and he could feel the softness of her mouth against his. "I want to do a good job for you."

And he wanted to— With rigid self-control he reined his wayward wants and tried to remember why he'd come in here in the first place.

"You will. You are. It's just that—" What? What was it he wanted to know?

He wanted to know a lot more than he would allow himself to think about.

Oh yes. Now he remembered.

Slowly, he loosened his white-knuckle grip on the counter and pushed away, leaving enough space between himself and his cook so that she could walk away from this encounter at any time. He'd had no business trapping her against the counter that way. What was the matter with him?

"You'll be taking care of my son," he said.

"A delight I'm looking forward to."

There she went with her fancy talk. "Right, but he's my son. It's my job to protect him."

She got that stricken look again as if he'd slapped her. "I would never do anything to hurt Gavin."

He believed her, but common sense said he needed more information about his housekeeper. "Why are you here, Jenna?"

"I required employment. You offered me a job."

"I don't mean here at Southpaw. I mean here in Texas. You have a new baby. Where is your family? Why aren't you with them? Won't they be concerned about you?"

The sadness that overcame her was a punch in his gut. Her bottom lip quivered. She looked down at her clenched hands. "Sophie's father died in rather embarrassing circumstances. Humiliating for me anyway."

A gentleman wouldn't press but Dax had to. "Meaning?"

She hesitated. And then sighed.

"At the time of the accident Derek was…my husband was…" Color drained from her face while she struggled to say the words. She twisted her fingers until the knuckles whitened. Until Dax had the insane urge to take her hands in his and calm her obvious stress.

"Never mind," he said. "I don't need details."

She looked up, her voice a whisper. "Thank you. It's difficult to discuss."

He got the picture. Her husband had cheated on

her and died in the process. Either that or he was a criminal killed during the commission of a felony. The last thought gave him pause, but even if it was true he didn't believe for a minute that Jenna was involved. She might be running from something, but not that.

"How did you end up here?"

"I wanted to escape the memories and raise my daughter away from the gossip and the painful past. Texas was an accident."

Dax watched as she twisted her hands over and over again until the whiteness reddened. Whatever she'd left behind had hurt her badly. He knew that kind of pain and the need to escape. Jenna Garwood was a kindred spirit, someone who understood the hurt that came from loving too much.

His voice gentled. "How was Texas an accident, Jenna?"

"I thought I had more time to find a place and get settled before Sophie's arrival."

"But Sophie had other plans."

Her face went soft, full of love for her child. "Yes. Once she arrived, I had to find work and a place to live immediately. A baby changes everything."

How well he knew. But at least, he'd had the ranch and a job and plenty of money to take care of Gavin. He could hire help. Jenna was alone with a newborn to support and no place else to go.

But one thought nagged him. "You're not the type to do this kind of work."

"Not the type?"

"Too educated or refined or…I don't know how to explain it but it's pretty clear you don't fit."

A determined glint flickered through her eyes. "I will do whatever is required to care for my daughter. At this point in time, domestic work allows me to be with her while earning a living. That's important to me. Regardless of my background, I am more grateful for this job than you can ever imagine."

His respect for the tough little mama ratcheted higher. What an amazing woman. He burned with an irrational need to pull his housekeeper into his arms and promise to care for her and Sophie.

Dumb. Real dumb.

Yet he had plenty of money. He could assure they lacked nothing. He could support and protect and befriend. He could take care of them both while Jenna mothered her child and his son.

Don't be an idiot, Dax. Women are trouble. Remember?

Finally, to quiet the noise in his head, he muttered, "I'm sorry for all you've been through."

Her chin hitched higher. "Don't be. Sophie and I are delighted with our new environment. It is absolutely perfect. That is, if maintaining my employment and residence here will be a satisfactory arrangement for you and Gavin."

Dax's mouth quivered. She was really cute when she talked like that. Cute and sexy.

Blast his brain! He bit down on the inside of his cheek to punish himself. She wasn't sexy. She was a kid. A new mother in need of help.

But somewhere in the back of that blasted brain a voice laughed at his protestations.

Before he could blurt something foolish and regrettable Gavin came around the corner of the cabinets. A hint of cheese rimmed the boy's lips. He took one look at the adults and slapped his hands onto his hips. "Are you two gonna talk all day or eat dessert? A kid could starve around here."

CHAPTER SEVEN

"MISS JENNA, are you gonna read me a story?"

Jenna sat in the padded rocking chair next to the baby crib, soft lamplight glowing golden around her and Sophie. She glanced up at the small, dark-haired boy standing uncertainly in the door of the nursery.

"Come in, Gavin."

Clad in cartoon image pajamas, the child crept closer. "I got a book in my room."

Jenna's arms and back ached as never before but she couldn't refuse Gavin's request. After all, she was his employee. Caring for him was her responsibility. More than that, she felt an empathy with the child that she couldn't articulate. And she *had* promised a story.

"Do you mind if I bring Sophie along? She's having her dinner now." She dipped her chin to indicate the bottle in the baby's mouth.

He edged closer, hands behind his back, watching in fascination as Sophie's mouth tugged greedily at the nipple. "Is that all she eats?"

"For now. When she's older she'll take cereal and baby food."

"Babies don't got no teeth, do they?"

Jenna hid a smile at the atrocious grammar but intentionally emphasized the correction. "No, babies haven't any teeth."

"Can't you buy her some from the dentist? My Grandpa Joe got some there."

The inner smile moved outward. "She'll grow her own in a few months. Just wait and see." Assuming she and Sophie were still here in a few months.

So far her mother hadn't discovered her whereabouts, and on a ranch this remote, perhaps she wouldn't. Someday Jenna hoped to be strong enough to stand up against her parents, but she never had been before. Even now, with hundreds of miles between them, she went weak and shaky at the idea of going head-to-head with the formidable Elaine Carrington.

Sophie's bottle emptied with a sucking sound. Jenna lifted the baby to her shoulder and patted the tiny back.

Gavin remained at her side, one small hand resting on the arm of the chair.

"She burped," he announced. "Can she say 'Scuse me?"

What an adorable little boy. "Not yet, but when the time comes, I hope you'll help her learn your nice manners."

Gavin's chest puffed with importance. "I will. I promise. I know how to say 'scuse me." He turned his head and emitted a pretend belch and then whipped around with a proud grin. "'Scuse me please, ma'am."

Jenna laughed. "You are excused. Thank you very much."

"Gavin!" Dax's voice rang from the living room. "Time for bed."

One hand supporting Sophie's back, Jenna rose. "Your dad's calling. Let's read that story and get you tucked in."

"Okay!" Gavin took off like a Thoroughbred in the Kentucky Derby.

Jenna followed behind more slowly. Her body yearned for a hot bath and a long slumber.

As she passed through the living room, she paused. Her employer was kicked back in a burgundy recliner that had been drawn too close to the television. He had to know she was in the room, but he chose to ignore her.

Dax Coleman was a puzzling man. One minute he was brusque and crabby. The next he was kindness itself.

The encounter in the kitchen after dinner had shaken her in the oddest manner. Dax had been angry and demanding at first, and then some other emotion had flashed from him that had set her heart to thundering and her belly aquiver. The sparks had almost ignited her hair.

After Gavin's timely interruption, Dax had abruptly withdrawn. Yet their conversation had given her hope that she and her employer would get along. He'd even helped clear the table and put dishes in the washer, gruffly chastising her for overdoing.

Yes, *puzzling* was the word. For all his bluster, perhaps he was, as Crystal had indicated, one of the good guys. He just had a hard time letting anyone know.

She cleared her throat.

A commercial danced across the television screen. The furniture in this room was lovely if badly arranged. To see Dax's face, she had to walk around the chair and stand between him and the television.

"Gavin wants a story. Would you care to join

us?" He was the boy's father. Most likely, they shared a bedtime ritual.

Dax squinted in her direction. At some point, he'd run a hand through his longish hair and it stuck up in front. His five o'clock shadow had deepened to a real need for a shave. The quivery feeling returned to her belly and this time she recognized it for what it was. Attraction. Crystal Wolf was right about this, too. Dax Coleman looked delicious. Rumpled, relaxed, and delicious.

Oh dear. The last time she'd been attracted to a man had resulted in disaster.

She pressed a hand to her stomach. Dax followed the motion; a muscle in his jaw twitched before he abruptly turned back to the television.

"Tell Gavin I'll be in later to say good-night."

So that was that.

By the time she reached Gavin's room he had crawled beneath a blue dinosaur comforter and sat with his back bolstered by two fat pillows.

"Sit here." He patted the spot next to him. "I can hold Sophie if you want me to."

Jenna smiled. "You are very thoughtful, but I think I can manage." With Sophie in the crook of her elbow, she picked up a book with the opposite hand. Already she was learning that mothers need three arms. "Is this the story you want?"

"Yep." He propped his hands behind his head. "That's the one."

Jenna rested the baby along her thighs before stroking a hand over the book's colorful cover. "*Peter Rabbit*. I remember this from when I was a little girl."

"Did your mommy read it to you?"

Jenna's chest clutched. "No."

"Mine, neither. I don't have a mom." He said the words in a manner-of-fact tone, but Jenna sorrowed for what he'd missed. At least she'd had a mother on the premises, though Elaine Carrington was not one to dirty her hands with the day-to-day details such as story-reading. A Carrington daughter was a collector's doll to be taken out of the box in pristine condition, displayed briefly at meals or recitals, and returned to the care of servants, not to be seen or heard until the next time. Without the kindness of nannies she'd likely never have heard a bedtime story.

She was determined this would not happen to Sophie.

With a lump in her throat she began to read. By page three Gavin had scooted until his body pressed against her side, bringing with him the pleasant smell of soap and toothpaste. She circled his shoulders with one arm, displaying the book so he could see the pictures. He sighed his approval, leaned closer and grasped the book's edge with one hand.

When the story ended, he said, "I'm glad Peter Rabbit escaped, aren't you, Miss Jenna?"

"Indeed."

"But he shouldn't have gone in the garden. His mama told him not to. Right?"

"Exactly right. Children should always obey their parents." She almost choked on the words. She had always obeyed her parents until Derek.

She closed the book and placed it on the stand next to Gavin's bed. When she turned back, the little boy was looking at the baby in her lap. Tentatively, with surprising gentleness, he touched the top of Sophie's hand with one finger.

"Miss Jenna?"

"Yes?"

"Are you and Sophie going to stay here for always?"

"I don't know."

She could see the answer troubled him. "I hope you stay a long time."

"Why is that?"

"So Sophie can be my baby sister. Noah has a baby brother. I want a baby, too, but Daddy says no. He says we'd have to get a mama to have a baby and he's not ever getting us another mama. So if you stay, Sophie can be my sister."

The child's words were a revelation into the father. Whatever had happened between Dax and his ex-wife cut deep. So much so that he feared getting hurt again, a fear Jenna understood completely.

No wonder Dax Coleman appeared kind and angry all in one package.

The dark-haired boy touched her heart, too. He longed for siblings and probably a mother, as well. Rough and tumble, timid and gentle at the same time, Gavin would be an easy child to love. The notion brought an ache to her chest. Where was his mother? What could have been so terrible about her life here at Southpaw that she would leave this precious, handsome son?

Even though Sophie was little more than a week old, Jenna knew she'd miss her more than life if they couldn't be together.

"Are you ready to have the lights out now?"

"I didn't say my prayers yet."

"All right then. Say them."

Squeezing his eyes closed, Gavin clasped his hands together beneath his chin. Jenna listened as he recited the "Now I lay me" prayer and went through a litany of God blesses before proclaiming with a sigh, "Amen." His eyes sprang open. "Can I have a drink?"

To her surprise, Dax stepped into the room. "He'll do this all night if you let him."

Gavin batted thick black eyelashes. "I'm thirsty, Daddy."

Dax relented with a half chuckle, half sigh. "Go on then. Get your drink, but nothing else."

Gavin scampered off the bed and disappeared. Jenna could hear him rattling around in the bathroom next door.

Dax glanced toward the noise, the hint of a smile on his face. "You read good."

The comment came out of nowhere. "What?"

"*Peter Rabbit*. Read in your voice, he took on a whole different personality."

"Well, thank you, I think." She offered a smile. "You were welcome to come in."

How long had he been standing in the hallway?

"Didn't want to disturb you." He shifted and cast another glance toward the bathroom and the sound of running water and clinking glass. "I need to say something."

Jenna tensed. "Have I done anything wrong?"

He made an irritated sound and swatted the air. "No. Not you. Me. I came on too strong in the kitchen. I apologize."

Relief surged like Hawaiian surf. "You have every right to know about the people in charge of your son."

His mouth twisted. "Don't let me off the hook that easy."

"All right, then." She pointed a finger at him. "Consider yourself appropriately castigated."

Dax surprised her with a laugh. "Castigated. That'll teach me to behave."

Jenna found herself sharing a smile with her employer. He was really handsome when he smiled. She took the thought captive and stowed it away.

"Dax, you have my solemn promise. I will care for Gavin as I will Sophie. With everything in me. You must never, ever be concerned that I would give anything less than my best to your son."

He gave a curt nod. "Can't ask for more than that. He's all I have, you know. He's—"

"Everything." Jenna finished the thought for him, intuitively understanding the depth of his feelings—because she felt the same about Sophie. "Your child is everything."

"Yeah," he said, shifting from one boot to the other. "Everything."

That one spark of kinship ignited a glow in Jenna's heart. Dax Coleman loved his son the way she loved Sophie. And that was a beautiful thing to know about a man. He loved deep. He loved strong. And forever.

The revelation shook her. She'd only just arrived and was the man's employee. She had no right to think of him as a…friend. As a man.

But she did.

Stunned by the emotion splashing around inside like a raft on the Colorado rapids, she stroked Sophie's sleeping face with one finger, thinking.

Dax's gravelly voice scraped across the silence, quiet and dangerously attractive. "She's a good baby, isn't she?"

"I think so, but I haven't been around babies much, so I have no one to compare."

He cocked to one side, resting his weight on a hip. The tension from earlier tonight had inexplicably dissipated. Puzzling man. Fascinating man.

"No nieces or nephews?"

Jenna shook her head and met his gaze. "I was an only child."

"Are your parents still living?"

She could hear the unasked question. If they're still alive, why aren't you with them? Wouldn't they want to know about their grandchild? She focused her attention on Sophie's fingers, lifting the tiny digits up one by one, unable to look her employer in the eye.

"No. They're dead." At least to her, but her pulse rattled at the lie. "Yours?"

"Dad's gone. Mom moved to Austin some years back to be near my sister, Karina. Once in a while they drive up here or I take Gavin to see them. Not as often as I'd like. Life's busy."

"What about Christmas? Won't you see them then?"

"I don't know yet. Haven't given it much thought."

The holiday was only weeks away. "Doesn't Gavin have a list a mile long?"

"Two miles." He smiled again.

"Who's Grandpa Joe?"

Dax chuckled. "Gavin's good buddy and my ninety-two-year-old great-granddaddy. He's in a care facility over in Saddleback, feeble as a kitten but sharp as a tack."

Gavin wandered back into the room. "Grandpa Joe is my best friend." He hopped onto the bed, his little body slithering beneath the comforter. Water glistened on his hair and around his mouth. He'd apparently combed his hair as well as having that final drink. "I'm ready. Tuck me in."

Dax stepped to the bedside and bent low, pulling the boy into a hug before settling him again with the covers tucked snugly beneath the small chin. "'Night, sport. Sleep tight."

"'Night, Daddy. Don't let the bedbugs bite. 'Night, Miss Jenna."

"Good night, Gavin. Sweet dreams."

Dax gave the child one final pat on the chest and straightened, turning for the door. Jenna, baby in arms, moved past him and started down the hall. As the light snapped out, she heard Gavin's voice one last time. "See, Dad? Having a mama in the house isn't so bad after all."

Dax knew he was dreaming, but the knowledge didn't stop the parade of emotions. In his dream, Gavin was still a baby and he was an exhausted, confused single dad, asleep in his half-empty king-size bed, wishing his wife would come home and help with the baby. And Gavin was crying. Demanding a bottle. Screaming for the mother that would never come.

Dax burrowed deeper into the pillow. Sometimes if he let the baby cry for a few minutes, they could both go back to sleep. After all, he was dreaming. The dream would end, along with the deep ache of regret and the incessant crying.

The cries grew louder.

Reba's mocking face flickered through the dream like a ghost. Ignoring her son's tears, she danced before Dax with a flowy scarf over her face, laughing as she looped arms with another man and flitted away with only a parting glance at her devastated husband and crying child.

The sorrow in Dax's gut turned to acid. He hadn't had this dream in years. He needed to wake up.

Thrashing against the tangle of covers, he fought off sleep and sat upright. A film of sweat covered his body, and his chest heaved, but he forced his breathing to calm. He'd long ago stopped loving Reba. Why had he dreamed about her tonight?

A mewling cry from the far back of the house was his answer.

A baby *was* crying. Gavin? He shook his head.

No, couldn't be. The baby was Sophie. Jenna's pink baby doll was crying.

Still mired in a kind of half sleep with cobwebs in his brain, he threw his feet onto the floor and padded down the hall toward the sound.

The house was dark except for the glow of a three-quarter moon splashing pale whiteness across the carpet. Dax needed no other light to maneuver in his own home. Even the nursery, as little as he'd used those rooms, was familiar. The baby's room had two entries, one from inside Jenna's bedroom and the other from the hall. He quietly pushed open the hallway door and stepped to the crib.

Sophie squirmed within the tight confines of a soft, thick blanket, her cries frantic now. Dax bent low, scooped the bundle into his large hands and lifted her against his naked chest. She was a feather, a dandelion puff, so light and fragile.

As he started out of the nursery toward the kitchen and the supply of formula he'd seen in the refrigerator, the tile was cold against his bare feet. The cooled atmosphere of the house sent prickles over his flesh. He came fully awake.

His heart slammed against his rib cage. This baby creating a single spot of warmth on his chest was not Gavin. This was Sophie, not his child. She was not his responsibility.

The infant whimpered, her head turning this way and that in search of food.

Jenna must be dead tired not to have heard the baby cry. But what did he expect? He'd worked her like a field hand from the very first day, expecting her to clean house, care for Gavin, do the shopping, cook his meals, clean the kitchen and still have the energy to get up at two o'clock with a newborn.

He'd even sent her to town for groceries that second day. She'd come back all rosy and chattery, talking about how much fun she'd had— in the grocery store no less. Picking out cantaloupe and watermelon and showing off Sophie to everyone in the place. He remembered how that worked. Carrying a baby into the grocery store in Saddleback was the same as throwing a party with free food. Everyone came running. He smiled at the memory.

Jenna had reacted to the trip with unbridled enthusiasm, as if she'd never shopped for groceries in her life. She was the same way about everything, come to think of it.

The ranch house was starting to respond to her enthusiasm.

But the truth was Jenna had been at the Southpaw for nearly a week now without a break, working hard enough to drive her into exhaustion.

He was an inconsiderate jerk.

Working in the semidark kitchen, he heated the baby bottle with one hand while holding Sophie securely with the other as he'd done dozens of times with Gavin. "Let your mama sleep, Sophie girl. Uncle Dax will fix you right up."

Okay, so he wasn't her uncle, but he felt like one. He'd been with her from the get-go. Not that he dared let himself get too close. No use getting in an emotional tangle about a baby destined to move on. A woman like Jenna wouldn't be here long. Once on her feet, she'd find a better job. She'd move on to a city somewhere with people of her education and breeding. Even a fool like him recognized quality and class when he saw it. Reba had no class at all, and even she hadn't stayed—which told him a lot about his shortcomings.

Sophie squirmed and let out a howl. Dax grunted away the useless, self-despising thoughts. He wouldn't let himself get attached, but right now, only a heartless jerk could ignore the cries of a hungry infant.

The microwave beeped. Dax took the bottle, shook a drop onto his wrist, then slid the warm nipple into the seeking, rosebud mouth. The crying stopped instantly to be replaced by the small, humming sounds an infant makes at feeding time. He'd always liked that sound. Relieved. Contented.

Padding barefoot back to the nursery, he thought about snapping on the lamp but decided against it. No use disturbing Jenna. He moved to close the door between the nursery and the bedroom beyond. As he did, he caught a glimpse of Jenna in the moonlight, curled on her side, sleeping like a rock. Her hair was down, spread across the pillow in spiky shadows. He could hear the soft hush of her breathing.

She didn't even stir.

He'd looked in this room many times before when Gavin was tiny and always found it empty. There was something renewing, redeeming even, to have a mother there now, steps away from her child. It eased the tight hard knot in his soul the tiniest bit.

He feasted on the feeling for several seconds,

experiencing a connection with Jenna Garwood that he couldn't explain or fully comprehend.

Then, quietly, he shut the door.

CHAPTER EIGHT

JENNA AWOKE WITH A JERK and sat straight up in bed. Daylight streamed through the window. From down the hall came the sounds of people moving around and the undecipherable rumble of conversation. She'd overslept.

Leaping from the bed, she rushed into the nursery. Sophie was gone, her covers tossed aside. The changing table was in disarray. Had she been crying? Had Dax, annoyed by the noise, been forced to tend his employee's child?

Heart thudding, she quickly dressed and headed for the kitchen. Heretofore, she'd risen at six to have breakfast on the table before Gavin's school bus rumbled to a stop at seven.

Things had been going so well up until now, but her mother regularly fired employees for tardiness. Would Dax do the same?

She rushed into the kitchen only to be drawn

up short. Dax, barefoot and shirt front unbuttoned, stood over the stove turning bacon with a long fork. Gavin sat at the table dressed for school, hair combed, his face washed and shiny. And Sophie lay in her carrier in front of the little boy. Gavin gently tweaked her onesie-clad toes and shook a rattle above her face. Her eyes, still unable to fully focus, crossed from the effort.

"I'm so sorry," she gushed. "Please forgive me."

Dax offered the long fork. "Save me quick before I create a disaster."

She grabbed an apron from inside a cupboard and tied it around her waist. "Aren't you angry?"

"About?" He offered the fork again. She took it, reached around him, turned the burner down and the range vent on.

"I overslept. This is my job." She poked at the bacon. The crispy strips of pork were nearly done. "I'm supposed to have breakfast on the table by now."

He shrugged. "You were tired."

Fatigue was never an excuse. Domestics executed their duties or found other employment.

"I can't apologize enough."

"You'd better not apologize again." His tone was low and dangerous.

Her pulse skittered. She turned her attention from the bacon to her employer. He was impossibly close, his broad chest naked, the stubble of unshaved beard roguish and attractive. This man who'd taken care of her hungry daughter, started breakfast, dressed Gavin for school and wasn't even upset to have done so.

Since that first night when she'd felt the tug of attraction, she tried to maintain a professional if friendly distance, but this morning, after his incredible kindness, she was especially aware of his appeal. He wasn't classically handsome like Derek but he oozed rugged, masculine sex appeal. And he didn't seem to know it.

She hadn't thought about her appearance in a long time but suddenly she wished she were prettier. Though she'd gained little weight with Sophie, she wished her body was toned and tanned and sexy. The thought made her want to cry. She'd never been sexy. If she had been, her husband wouldn't have found another woman before the ink was dry on their marriage license.

Sophie made a fussy sound. Before she could react, Gavin poked the pacifier into the baby's mouth. Jenna rewarded him with a smile and then went back to the bacon, lifting the strips out of the pan and onto a plate.

Enough thoughts of sex appeal. She was here to do a job, to provide for her child, not moon over her employer's pectorals. And she was already running late.

"Sophie must have slept through the night," she said, scuttling about the kitchen, quickly taking breakfast items from the refrigerator and cupboards. "I'm sure that's why I overslept. After her two o'clock feeding, I'm usually half-awake until the alarm rings at five-thirty."

Dax leaned his jean-covered behind against the counter and crossed his arms over the appealing chest, expression amused. "Not."

She paused, carton of milk in hand. "What?"

"Sophie didn't sleep through the night. Just her mama."

The milk carton plunked onto the table. "You mean?" Dax had gotten up with her in the middle of the night? "Oh Dax, I'm so—"

Before she could apologize again, he lifted a finger in warning. "Uh-uh. Careful there. A tired mama needs rest. I was already awake. No need troubling you. Sophie and I did all right."

The tension in her shoulders relaxed. He really wasn't angry. "I suppose my brilliant daughter recognized a true expert while I, on the other hand, am still a novice, struggling much of the time to get her diaper on frontward."

Dax grinned. Oh my. He was luscious when he smiled. The tiny lines of weathering crinkled white near his eyes and increased his craggy attractiveness.

Aware she was staring, she spun toward the counter where boxed pancake mix awaited. Thank goodness, she'd had the good sense and had spent enough time researching on the Internet to understand the value of prepackaged goods. She wondered if the Carrington cooks had ever been allowed to use such conveniences. Knowing Elaine, probably not.

"She's a greedy little kitten," Dax was saying. "She likes her bottle right on time." He bumped against her side. "Need any help here?"

"Would you mind pouring juice?" Beating the lumpy batter, she glanced at the clock. "Gavin's time is running out."

The boy piped up. "I could stay home, Miss Jenna. Help you out around here."

Batter sizzled against the hot pan, sending up a

wave of scent and heat. Jenna and Dax exchanged amused glances.

"You're exceedingly gracious to offer, Gavin, but your education is far too important. May I count on your help on Saturday?"

Gavin's forehead puckered. "After cartoons?"

Dax, a cup of coffee to his lips, sputtered with laughter. Jenna giggled. "After cartoons will do nicely. Thank you."

She slid the hot pancakes onto a plate which she set in front of Gavin while simultaneously scooting Sophie's carrier out of the way. The baby once again dozed, undisturbed by the sights and sounds swirling around her.

"Eat, sweetheart," she said to Gavin. "The bus will arrive soon."

She spun back to the stove to drip more batter onto the pan. Cooking breakfast required perfect timing. Most mornings she worked for a healthier offering, including breakfast casseroles and fruit compotes. One day of pancakes and bacon wouldn't hurt.

Dax had just poured a tooth-decaying amount of warm syrup onto a stack of pancakes when his cell phone chirped.

He made a disparaging face before barking into the mouthpiece. "What?"

After listening for a minute, he said, "Will anyone die if I eat breakfast first?"

Then he tossed the telephone onto the table and went back to his pancakes.

The short comment was exactly the kind she'd come to expect of her employer. He didn't waste words, which made him all the more difficult to understand.

Jenna refilled his coffee cup. As she turned away, he caught her wrist in his long fingers. "Sit down. Your pancakes are getting cold."

The touch of Dax's hard fingers against her skin brought a strange hum to her nerve endings.

She'd learned not to argue about taking meals with the family. He was insistent. She had to admit she preferred meals with the reticent rancher and his shyly sweet son to being alone. Very slowly, she was getting to know the nice man behind the glower. Getting close was another, more troubling matter.

"May I please get a glass of milk first?" she asked, glancing down at the circle of fingers where he held her captive.

He hissed through his teeth, dropped her hand and attacked his pancakes with an almost angry force.

Jenna turned away in confusion. What was that

all about? Had he felt the staggered trip of her pulse against those thick, calloused fingers? Had he recognized the buzz of electricity racing through her blood and been repelled?

She had no right feeling attracted to her employer. She'd lose her job. He'd toss her out. Worse, she was no judge of men. Hadn't she learned a thing after the fiasco with Derek?

Drawing upon a lifetime of pretending everything was all right when it wasn't, she poured a glass of milk and sat down, intent on making normal conversation. Executing appropriate small talk was a fine art, her mother would say, and though she was less skilled than her mother, she could manage.

"Problems on the ranch?" she asked, indicating the discarded cell phone.

Dax glowered at the device, though Jenna wondered if the scowl was meant for her. "Rowdy can handle the situation until I get there. That's what I pay him for."

Rowdy. The thought of Dax's top ranch hand soured the sweet taste of pancakes. For more than a week she'd managed to avoid another encounter with the man, a run of good luck she hoped would continue.

"What's wrong? A sick animal?" Beyond the subtleties of preparing a lovely prime rib, Jenna knew nothing about cattle. Dax had told her a little about the ranch, enough that she was interested. For a woman who'd been sheltered from so much, she wanted to know everything about everything.

"We have an A-I crew here today. They're early." He forked a bite of syrupy pancake and stirred it around his plate.

"May I inquire as to what an A-I crew might be?"

His mouth twitched. "You may. Artificial insemination."

Jenna was certain she turned pink. "I never realized such a thing occurred in cattle."

"Just one select group of experimental cows."

"Experimental cows. How fascinating." Not that she had any idea what he was talking about, but she liked the rumble of that scratchy-rough voice. And she felt rather pleased to have drawn him out. Most mornings, he mumbled hello and goodbye and disappeared out the door. Evenings were somewhat better.

Apparently, she'd been asking the wrong questions because once he started talking about his experimental cows, he didn't stop. Some of the conversation about selective breeding of a certain pasture of purebred cattle went completely over her head, but she listened hard. Dax Coleman was passionate about two things: his son and this ranch.

During a pause, Jenna noticed the clock. "Gavin, you need to brush your teeth. The bus will be here in five minutes." When Gavin scooted away from the table, she turned back to Dax. "Now tell me more about Number Thirty-two and what made her special enough to win 'Supreme Overall Breed' at the San Antonio show?"

Dax pointed his fork at her. "Do you really want to hear this or are you just being your perky self?"

Perky? Was that a compliment?

"I'm learning the nuances of ranch life," she said. "Please continue."

Dax shook his head. "The nuances of ranch life, huh? Okay, you asked for it." He launched into a technical explanation that had her mentally galloping to keep up. Dax Coleman might be a rough cattle rancher but he was a very bright man.

By the time Gavin returned, dragging his camo schoolbag, they'd turned the topic to horses and winter wheat pasture.

"I had no idea there was so much involved in raising cattle."

"Most folks think you turn 'em out to pasture and forget about them."

She smiled. "I can tell by the hours you put in that there is more to the work than that."

Gavin sidled up to his father for a goodbye hug.

"See ya tonight, sport. Be good."

Then the little boy headed toward her. She zipped his coat before pulling him in for a hug. Gavin had won her heart the first night with his precocious charm and obvious need for motherly attention. He seemed to crave her hugs and she was quickly growing to crave his, as well. Gavin was a sweet and gentle child.

She inhaled his clean, school-ready scent before turning him loose.

"Miss Jenna," he said, rustling inside his schoolbag. "I forgot to show this to you."

"What is it?"

He pushed a note in front of her, his face a picture of hope. "Can you make cupcakes for my snack? I told Miss Baker you could. You're a real good cooker."

The compliment brought a smile. Gavin was such a dear little boy with such eagerness to please. Sometimes Dax grew impatient with the child's anxieties, but they touched Jenna's heart.

She understood, empathized even, with being afraid. She'd been afraid most of her life.

Thankfully, he'd volunteered her cooking skills and nothing else. The kitchen was the only place she felt comfortable, but so far Dax had not complained about her mistakes in other areas. Like the pink socks. She wondered if he'd noticed those yet?

She shot a quick, relieved glance at his bare feet. She wasn't certain what she'd done wrong yesterday with the laundry but she suspected Gavin's bright red T-shirt was the culprit. Next time she'd separate the colors.

"I would be delighted to bake cupcakes, Gavin. When do you need them?"

With a shrug, the boy bent to zip his schoolbag. "It says on the note. I forget."

Jenna perused the note. "Oh dear."

Dax leaned to peer over her shoulder "What?"

Jenna refused to acknowledge the tingle of awareness where he brushed against her. "Today is Gavin's snack day."

Gavin's hope melted down his face like candle wax. Dax took one glance at his son and his own expression hardened. To Jenna he said, "Forget it then. It's too much trouble. If I have time I'll run into town to the bakery."

"But I wanted Noah to see the baby," Gavin protested.

"Son, don't make promises that aren't yours to keep." His tone was unyielding, angry even, though Jenna couldn't comprehend the reason.

The boy's mouth quivered. "Miss Jenna likes me. I thought—"

A nerve twitched in Dax's jaw. "I'll send your teacher a note and let her know you made a mistake."

The dejected child dropped his head.

"Gentlemen, please!" Jenna slapped down her napkin and rose. "May I speak for myself?"

At the startled glances of both males, she proceeded. "Though I lack the tools for anything artistically decorative, I want to provide refreshments for Gavin's class. I was only lamenting the lack of a pastry bag and tips, not refusing the task. Okay?"

Gavin, bewildered and uncertain, blinked from Jenna to Dax and back again. "Does that mean you'll bring cupcakes?"

In spite of themselves, the adults looked at Gavin and then at each other…and burst out laughing.

CHAPTER NINE

HUMMING A HAPPY TUNE, Jenna shoved at the enormous leather sofa parked directly in the path of the dining room and the gorgeous stone-and-wood fireplace. While Gavin's cupcakes cooled and Sophie watched from her musical swing, Jenna had decided to do something about this ill-arranged living room. As lovely as the design was, the furniture was not being utilized effectively and the result was an unattractive and less-than-comfortable space.

She could actually imagine throwing a wonderful party in this house, maybe for Christmas or New Year's Eve. She already had her eye on some fabulous holiday decorations at the local hobby store and later today, she planned to explore Dax's storage building for others. But first, this space needed rearranging to reach its full potential of design and beauty.

With a groan of effort, she managed to scoot the sofa a few inches. Straining with all her strength while murmuring about her skinny arms, she didn't hear the door open.

"What do you think you're doing?"

At the sound of Dax's furious voice, Jenna jumped and spun around.

He stood, stance wide, hair windblown, looking like a thunderhead.

A hand pressed to her thudding heart, Jenna said, "Dax. I didn't hear you come in."

"Apparently." He slapped both fists low on his hips, billowing out the sides of a sheepskin jacket. "Answer me. What are you doing?"

"Rearranging." She bit her bottom lip. This was the first time he'd objected to any of her changes. She'd washed and moved curtains, re-arranged pictures, added touches of color and interest with items she'd discovered in boxes in the garage. She'd even added a Christmas wreath to the front door and bowls of apple-scented pot-pourri to the tables. Last night, he commented on how good everything smelled and she'd been giddy with pleasure.

Now he was angry. And she had no idea why.

"You have no business moving furniture."

"I'm sorry. I thought you wouldn't mind."

"Well, I do."

"All right then." She pushed at the end of the sofa, edging the heavy item slowly back into the former position.

"Stop!"

She did. "Do you or do you not want this divan back where it was?"

"I don't give a rat's…behind where the couch is."

She blinked at her bewildering boss, lost until he continued.

"You'll hurt yourself. Show me where you want it. I'll move it."

"Oh." He was upset for her sake? Her insides turned to mush. Dax had the most unusual way of showing kindness. She touched his sleeve, surprised to feel the rigid muscle through all that cloth. "You're not angry because of the change in furniture, are you?"

"Why would I get mad about that? The place never looked better."

She smiled, her confidence soaring. Since taking this position, Jenna had discovered something about herself. She was actually good at many things her mother would consider below her station. She was good at them and she enjoyed them, too. She was starting to believe in herself in a way she'd never dreamed possible.

She was also learning some things about her employer. He struggled to express his true feelings, hiding his tender side behind bluster. But the evenings when he listened to her read to Gavin or helped his son with his homework, or even during those times she'd caught him in the nursery talking softly to Sophie, she'd learned the truth he tried to hide. He *was* a good guy. And Jenna was starting to like Dax Coleman. A lot.

"The fireplace should be the focal point of this room," she said. "So if we move the sofa there—" she pointed "—and a chair here and here, we'll open up the space and draw the eye to this beautiful stonework."

Dax contemplated momentarily. "I see your point."

"And the Christmas tree will be positively glorious there." She moved to the side of the fire-place, lifting her hands above her head in imitation of a tree. "See?"

"Couldn't ask for a prettier tree." Then as if he hadn't meant to say such a thing, he gave a curt nod. "Let's get it done."

But just the small hint that Dax thought she was pretty soothed an ache in Jenna's mind.

Biceps bulging and with barely any effort, he moved the furniture as she directed. Once she reached to help and he swatted at her with a growl. She hopped back, laughing, more confident now.

"You don't scare me."

Green eyes danced. "Then why'd you jump?"

She tossed a throw pillow at him. He caught it with one hand and growled again. "Careful, lady."

"Or what? The big bad wolf will get me?" She laughed, feeling free and a little excited.

Dax started toward her. "He might."

A delicious shiver raced up her spine. She grabbed another pillow, holding the square bit of fluff in the small space between them. Dax snatched the pillow away, advancing. With a squeal, Jenna wheeled away. Her heart thudded and her blood zinged. This was one big bad wolf she wouldn't mind being pursued by.

She glanced back. Dax loomed above her, arms raised, hands forming claws like a bear. He roared.

Jenna screamed and jerked to the side. Her calves encountered a table she'd just moved. She lost her balance and tumbled backward. Dax caught her upper arms and yanked. He was amazingly strong. She was propelled forward and slammed into his chest.

"Are you all right?" He glared down at her, green eyes glittering.

"You saved me." Teasing, she pitter-pattered a hand against his heart. "My hero."

She'd meant it as a joke, as part of the silly game they were playing, but as soon as she touched him, all frivolity fled. She was aware of her body pressed against his, aware that she liked the feel of his arms around her.

"Dax?" she said.

A muscle twitched below his eye. His nostrils flared. After a long aching moment in which Jenna thought—hoped—he might kiss her, his whole body tensed, he dropped his hold and took three steps back.

Without looking at her, he grabbed his hat and jammed it down on his head.

"Let me know if you need any more furniture moved."

He wheeled away and left her standing in the living room alone.

She was getting under his skin in the worst way.

Dax tied off the end of a barbed wire strand and

shoved his fencing pliers into his back pocket. For the last two hours, he'd been riding this fence line with Rowdy, checking for gaps, fixing spots and thinking about his housekeeper.

Though his body was warm from his labors, his face was cold. The shiny whiteness of the clouds along with a stiff north wind hinted at a weather change.

He hadn't slept fifteen minutes last night. Instead, he'd lain there in the dark thinking of how close he'd come to stepping over the line with Jenna. He'd never wanted to kiss anyone so much in his life. To kiss her. To hold her. Just to be with her.

To make matters worse, at least for him, after taking the cupcakes to Gavin's school, she'd returned bubbling over with chatter and goodwill. If she'd been affected by the near kiss she didn't let on. A man could get a complex. Not that he wanted her to think anything about that moment in his arms. Maybe she hadn't noticed. Maybe she hadn't been affected. Wouldn't that be for the best?

Right. Good. She'd gone to Gavin's school and had a great time. She'd forgotten all about his unfortunate lapse in judgment.

A shaft of wind slid down the back of his neck. He flipped his collar up.

From the way Jenna had behaved at dinner, you'd think she'd never been in a school building in her life. She'd been all giddy and thrilled to eat cafeteria food and have kindergartner's wipe snot on what he was certain was a very expensive skirt.

Something was going on with Gavin, too. Last night, he'd found the little dude playing quietly in the nursery. He claimed to be guarding baby Sophie so she wouldn't get scared. From a kid who'd always been scared of his own shadow, the gesture was a puzzle.

But then so was his housekeeper. A puzzle and a disturbance.

"Been meaning to ask you something, boss." Rowdy shot a cocky grin his way.

"Yeah?" Dax squinted toward the clouds gathering in the west. Maybe the wind would blow in some much-needed moisture. They'd been irrigating the winter wheat for weeks now.

"How's your new housekeeper working out?"

The question, given he couldn't get Jenna out of his head, caught him completely off guard. He gazed at the clouds another second before turning a squint-eyed gaze at Rowdy. "All right. Why?"

"Just wondering about her. She's single. Pretty. Curved in all the right places."

Dax studied his hand for a moment, not liking the direction of this conversation. "She's a new mother."

He stuck a foot in a stirrup and swung up into the saddle.

Rowdy looped a roll of wire over the saddle horn and guffawed. "You're getting old, Dax, if that's all you see."

Thirty-four sounded older every day, but Dax didn't much appreciate the reminder. And he sure wasn't going to tell Rowdy the truth.

"She's doing her job, cooks great food I've never heard of and looks after Gavin." The boy adored her, followed her like a pup hungry for her smiles and hugs. The behavior was pitiful if he thought about it, but he was glad to see Gavin happy.

Rowdy swung into the saddle and they urged the horses to a walk, examining fence line as they rode while keeping an eye out for strays. "What about you?"

Dax ruminated a beat. "What about me?"

"You know what I'm talking about. She taking good care of you, too?"

Dax didn't like Rowdy's implication, though he supposed no insult was intended. The young cowboy was comfortable with horses, cattle and women. Lots of women. Naturally, his roving eye would land on the only female within fifteen miles. What man with any juice in his veins wouldn't notice Jenna?

"She's a good employee."

Rowdy, holding the reins with a light hand, rose in his stirrups and twisted around, squinting toward a pond dam. "That's all?"

No.

"That's all." Dax heard the growl in his voice, felt the prickle of jealousy beneath his skin.

The saddle creaked as Rowdy settled in again. "Then I guess you won't mind if I stop by the house and pay my respects, maybe ask her out sometime."

Dax rubbed a sleeve across his face, more to avoid looking at his employee than to scratch an itch. What could he say without admitting that he was attracted to his too-young housekeeper? "She stays pretty busy."

"You can't work her 24-7, boss. Every woman likes a night out. Considering she had a kid, she's probably hankering to get away once in a while."

Dax bit down on his molars. Why hadn't he considered that?

As soon as the thought crossed his mind, he mentally kicked himself. He hadn't thought of it because he couldn't, no more than he could consider kissing her. Jenna was out of his league in more ways that one. "She's not your type, Rowdy. Leave her alone. There are plenty of girls in Saddleback waiting for you to call."

Rowdy didn't answer and they rode on, but Dax couldn't get the worry out of his head. He had no right to keep Jenna from having a life. She and that pink princess of hers needed a man to look after them, though she'd probably poison his potato frittata if she heard him say such a thing. Women were testy about that independence business nowadays. But Rowdy was probably right. She needed to get out, make friends, do things that young people do. Get away from the likes of him.

Maybe he should encourage a relationship between his housekeeper and his best ranch hand. Maybe if he did, he could stop thinking about her so much. About her fancy voice and her honey-brown eyes and kissable mouth. About the sweet way she catered to her baby—and his son. About her silvery laugh that caused a catch in his chest as though he couldn't quite breathe.

A cord of tension crept across his shoulders and up the back of his neck. He hoped he wasn't getting one of those headaches—blasted, debilitating things. They made him feel like some kind of sissy.

He kicked the horse into a trot and headed across pasture, leaving the other cowboy in the dust. The rush of wind in his face cleared his thinking.

He'd brought Jenna here to the Southpaw. She was his responsibility. Rowdy might be a good worker, but he was fast and loose with the ladies. Jenna deserved better than that.

Yesterday's near kiss was still on Jenna's mind as she bathed Sophie. She'd mulled over the incident off and on all day, finally coming to a conclusion. She had overreacted. Considering his normal behavior at dinner last night, Dax had already forgotten. Either that or he hadn't been about to kiss her at all.

She heard the back door open. A glance at the elephant clock on the armoire had her frowning. Dax hadn't come in for lunch and the time was long past, though he often skipped the noon meal in favor of work. But someone was certainly here now.

A quiver of concern passed over her. Was something wrong? Worse yet, had someone else come into the house?

Lifting Sophie from her tub, she wrapped the

slick little body in a soft, hooded terry cloth towel and went to find out.

Dax stood in the kitchen. He looked weary as he rummaged through the cabinets searching for something. Weary and masculine. She fought back the memory of those strong arms holding her.

"May I help you find something?" she asked. He'd tossed his hat on the counter along with his jacket. His hair was mussed, his shoulders tense. Body heat and cold air radiated from him.

"Aspirin." He rubbed the back of one hand over his eyes.

"Headache?"

He nodded, looking at her through bloodshot eyes with an expression of both embarrassment and suffering.

"I rearranged the cabinets," she said. "All medicines are now in the master bath out of Gavin's reach. I'll get the pain reliever."

Pressing Sophie's still damp body against her shoulder, she started in that direction. Dax followed. "I can manage."

She let him pass her in the hallway, noticing his usual cowboy swagger was more of a stagger. "Dax. You're sick."

She followed him into the master bath, squelching the hint of impropriety. "Go lie down. I'll get this."

He lifted one arm halfway then let it drop in surrender. "Thanks."

He staggered out of the bathroom. Jenna stared after him.

He really *was* sick. And she was worried. Dax was cowboy tough, almost stoic.

With Sophie in arms, balancing the aspirin and water was a trick, but she managed. By the time she entered the bedroom, Dax was sprawled, fully dressed on a massive brown-and-blue comforter. He levered up on one elbow to accept the medication, then eased back down. His eyes were barely focusing now and his forehead glistened with sweat.

Without giving the action much thought, she lay Sophie next to him and touched his forehead. His skin felt both hot and clammy. He shivered.

"Should I call the doctor?" she asked, growing more worried by the minute.

"No," he murmured. "Just close the blinds and keep Gavin quiet. I'll be fine."

"You aren't fine, Dax. You're really sick." Too sick to remove his dirty boots.

When she tugged them off, he didn't protest. Oh yes, he was definitely sick. She went into the bathroom and returned with a cool, damp cloth. Dax didn't open his eyes but as she placed the cloth over his forehead, he sighed.

"You might feel better undressed." Her face heated to say such a thing, but the man was miserable.

"Later." Voice weak, he lifted a weak hand. "Go."

Gathering Sophie, she did as he commanded, backing out slowly, her gaze on him as long as possible. What was wrong? What if something terrible happened to Dax? He wasn't one to complain and in fact, she'd noticed the way he shrugged off hurts such as Gavin's bloody nose and his own more recent run-in with an angry cow that had left him with a dislocated finger. With gritted teeth, he'd yanked the joint back into place, slapped some ice on it and never mentioned the accident again.

This was something worse than a dislocation.

Fretting, she dried and dressed Sophie and rocked her for a while. The presence of her daughter soothed her nerves. When Sophie fell asleep again, Jenna put her to bed and tiptoed across the long house to Dax's door.

Peeking through the crack she'd left, she saw a white rim around his lips and the frown of misery between his dark eyebrows.

When Gavin arrived home from school, she met him in the foyer with a finger to her lips. "Your daddy is not feeling very well, Gavin. We need to be extra quiet okay?"

Nodding sagely, the boy placed his schoolbag on the table and slid off his coat, taking special care to make no noise.

"Is it one of his headaches?" he whispered.

"Does your dad often suffer from bad headaches?"

"I can't remember what they're called. Grains, I think. Yeah, that's it. Dad calls them his grains. They're bad."

"Migraines?" she asked, amused at the child's misunderstanding.

The little face screwed up in sympathy. "You get 'em, too?"

"No, sweetheart. Thankfully, I have never suffered with the malady but I have encountered it." Her mother had them at convenient times. Somehow she doubted Dax's were the same. "Will you help me keep Sophie quiet in the nursery tonight so your daddy can recuperate?"

"Yep, but I got homework. The letter *E. E* is for *egg*."

"Very good. Can you think of anything else that starts with the sound of *egg?*"

"Elephant. Like that clock in Sophie's room." He screwed up his face. "*Elephant* and *egg* and *egg-cited*."

Jenna's lips twitched. *"Excited?"*

"Yep. The way I feel about Christmas. I'm getting a bulldozer and a dump trunk. We're having a party at school, too."

"You are?"

"Yep. Miss Jenna?" He pulled papers from his bag and carried them to the kitchen table. "Are you coming back to my school?"

"I have to ask your father about it, but I hope to." The day at Gavin's elementary school had been one of the most interesting and enjoyable times she could remember. She'd never been in a public school classroom. The sounds and smells and colorful decor had captivated her. She'd read with a group of children, listened to their adorable chatter, and after serving cupcakes had helped put them down on little mats for a rest. When the teacher had asked her about volunteering once a week, calling her a natural with the kids, she'd been flattered and promised to give the offer some thought. But the answer had to come from Dax. He paid her to be here at the ranch.

"Noah said you're pretty. He said Dad probably likes you." Head bent as he carefully traced the letter *E,* his voice innocent as a lamb, he said, "I told him yes. Dad likes you a lot. Maybe Sophie will be my sister now."

With a pang, Jenna patted his back and headed for the kitchen to prepare dinner. This was Gavin's obsession with having a sibling and nothing more.

She took the marinated beef from the refrigerator, pausing with one hand on the oven dial.

Did Dax like her? She hoped so. She liked her job, loved the beauty of this austere country and was falling fast for Gavin. Most of all, she was safe here. In the days since Sophie's birth, she'd traveled into Saddleback, shopped, had lunch with Crystal, all without hearing mention of the runaway heiress from Pennsylvania.

Her life here grew fuller and more fulfilling every day. She could easily think of Texas as home, and as long as she and her daughter were free of the smothering pressures of her former lifestyle, Jenna didn't care if she was a domestic forever.

As she prepared dinner, she helped Gavin with his work, praised as he practiced writing his name in a laborious hand. She couldn't help thinking this was what a normal family life should be.

When the meal was complete, she debated about disturbing Dax. In the end, she prepared a plate of the beef tournedos and covered it. Though he'd teased her this morning about serving him tornadoes for dinner, she'd looked forward to his reaction to the delicious recipe. But that would have to wait. When and if he felt like eating, his meal would be ready.

After dinner, Gavin asked permission to play with his cars and dinosaurs in Sophie's room. Jenna adjusted the nursery monitor to keep an eye on both children as she cleaned the kitchen. When she poured dishwasher detergent into the holder inside the machine, she grimaced. A few days ago, she'd made the mistake of using laundry detergent. The result had flooded the tile with soapsuds. Gavin had been gleeful over the turn of events and Dax had laughed. She pretended to have accidentally picked up the wrong box, but in truth, she hadn't known the difference. She knew now.

Drying her hands on a dish towel, she checked the monitor again and heard Gavin's voice quietly telling the sleeping Sophie about an incident at school. With a smile, Jenna headed toward the master bedroom to peek in on Dax. As she approached the door, she heard him groan.

She pushed the door open. His covers were a rumpled mess. His hair shot in a dozen directions as though he'd yanked at it in agony.

"Dax?" she whispered.

Bloodshot eyes opened, then closed again, but not before she saw the pain. Needing to help, she went to Dax's office and searched the Internet. The World Wide Web had been her salvation during these days of learning to be a domestic engineer. She liked that term. Now, she searched until she found simple techniques for alleviating the pain of a migraine.

Back in Dax's bedroom, she wet another cloth and replaced the warm one, then eased onto the edge of the bed. Without asking permission, she began to gently massage his temples.

His eyes fluttered open to look at her in glazed curiosity, but he was clearly in too much pain to say anything beyond, "That helps."

She continued the gentle, circular strokes, praying he would find relief. When he tugged at the neck of his shirt, Jenna said, "Would you be more comfortable out of these clothes? I would be happy to assist."

Well, perhaps not happy but willing. The idea of seeing Dax unclothed made her belly quiver.

His body tensed and she could see him holding his breath. Then he exhaled but didn't answer.

Bracing herself to do what was best for her employer, Jenna unbuttoned his shirt. He had a magnificent chest and shoulders. Any woman would notice. She had the craziest urge to smooth her palm over the curved pectorals and discover if they were as rock-hard as she suspected.

Her pulse hammered against her throat. Her fingers tingled at the touch of him. Foolish, silly woman. The man was ill.

With steely resolve, she pushed the sleeves over his shoulders and slid them down his arms. He grunted once. She paused, afraid she'd hurt him.

With the shirt discarded, Jenna drew a deep breath and reached for the silver belt buckle. A hand stopped her. Jenna's gaze flew up to meet his.

Nostrils flared, he grumbled, "I'll do this."

She nodded and backed toward the door. "If you need me…"

"In a minute."

Did that mean he wanted her to return? She

stepped outside the room, checked the portable monitor in her pocket to be sure the children were safe, and waited.

She heard rustling and footsteps, then the give of the bed. Her heart beat in her throat and she felt flushed. An embarrassing situation, no doubt, but there was more to her discomfort than that.

"Jenna." The word was slurred.

She reentered the room, finding Dax in string-drawn lounge pants and nothing else. He'd replaced the damp cloth, covering his eyes. His chest rose and fell with the effort of his movements.

Jenna stepped to the bed and reclaimed her place on the edge. Determined to help this man who had helped her, she placed the baby monitor within her line of vision and as gently as she knew how, began to massage his temples again.

"Rest," she whispered. "Relax."

He inhaled deeply and exhaled on a sigh.

She massaged until her fingers numbed and her wrists ached but she refused to stop. Dax hadn't abandoned her when the going had been rough with Sophie, and she would not abandon him.

After the longest time, the tension eased from Dax's body. His breathing grew deep and even. The furrow between his brows smoothed.

With a tenderness that shook her, Jenna let her fingers drift down his temples, over the whisker-roughened jaw where she paused at the corners of his remarkable mouth.

Relaxed in sleep, he looked young and vulnerable. And incredibly male.

Stunned at the tender feelings he aroused in her, Jenna quietly eased off the bed and slipped from the room.

CHAPTER TEN

THE DAWN HAD YET TO BREAK when Dax entered the kitchen, drawn there by the scent of fresh coffee. He felt washed-out but infinitely better, the rampaging pain but a fading nightmare.

As bad as the dream had been, there had been a good part, too. Jenna. Even in the fog of a migraine, he'd been aware of her soft hands touching him, easing the throb in his temples, sliding his shirt from his body. Had he not been so ill—well, he had been. Otherwise, she would not have taken such liberties.

Yet he remembered.

This morning, Jenna was nowhere to be seen, but from the looks of things she was up and busy, probably tending Sophie. From what he'd gathered, she rose with the baby around six and never let up again until bedtime. He'd seen the fatigue around her eyes, felt a twinge of guilt for working her so hard, but she never complained and any suggestion that she ease up seemed to trouble her. He didn't know why. There was no chance of her being fired, though he figured she didn't know that yet.

After last night, when she'd tended him like a baby, her job was safe for as long as she wanted it.

He was embarrassed at his weakness, but she'd responded with such genuine care. This morning would tell the tale, though. He would know when he looked in her eyes if she considered him less of a man. Reba had.

He poured a thick brown mug full of steaming brew, dumped in two spoons of sugar and stirred. His housekeeper was still a mystery. In the back of his mind a nagging voice claimed she hadn't come completely clean about her reasons for being here. Sometimes she seemed to be looking over her shoulder. Other times she embraced the mundane business of life with the exuberance of a child experiencing things for the first time.

But Dax didn't care where she'd come from or why she'd chosen to stay here. He was simply glad she had.

She'd figured out Gavin faster than a flea hops and the little dude responded like a dry sponge.

He was grateful, though his growing feelings for his housekeeper went deeper than gratitude. Every day he reminded himself that she was too young, too smart and pretty and refined. She was wise, too, as if she had an old soul.

With a grunt at his fanciful thoughts, he stepped to the sink and deposited the spoon there for later cleanup. The window over the sink looked out on the backyard and beyond to the barns and corrals and separating pens. The first shifting of dawn's white-pink light cast a halo over the peaceful, drowsy ranch.

The beauty had particular significance this morning now that the Coleman curse of migraines had run its course and he'd survived.

He loved gazing out at the land he'd purchased from the rest of his family. No one else loved the ranch the way he did. No one else could tolerate the long days and 24-7 demands of the cowboy life. Most of all no one wanted to live out here far from the rest of civilization.

Which brought him back to his housekeeper. She seemed to relish the place and even if the pleasure was an act, he'd take it. He'd found her in the horse barns one day, Sophie attached to her front like a baby monkey on some kind of sling thing. He'd been surprised to hear that she had equestrian skills as she called them and after watching her with the horses for a while, he'd believed her. He'd offered to let her ride sometime, refraining from actually offering to ride along with her. No use being stupid.

After Rowdy's comments, though, he was having second thoughts. As much as he liked his ranch hand, he didn't want Rowdy messing with Jenna. She was too sweet and tender and innocent. Rowdy was a rounder.

He sipped his coffee, sighed out his pleasure in such a simple thing as good coffee and sunrise, and leaned against the sink to watch. The silent sun shimmered just beneath the horizon, casting up hints of the coral and yellow to come. The morning sun was magical to him, bringing with it the promise of a new, clean day, uncluttered by yesterday's suffering.

He chuckled and shook his head. He was feeling poetic this morning.

From the corner of his eye he saw movement on the long, back porch and turned in that direction. A figure—Jenna—huddled beneath a blanket on the cedar bench he rarely used. Once, he'd planned for the backyard and patio to be a place for family and friends to gather, a place to watch his children play and grow. Those plans, like so many others, had died in their infancy.

After pouring a second cup of coffee complete with cream, the way Jenna liked it, he eased the back door open with his hip and joined her.

"Good mornin'," he said. Standing with legs wide he breathed in the crisp, clean morning. The air was still as death, though he knew the wind would get up later on. Winter encroached on the perfect fall.

"Good morning." Her voice was a soft melody, blending with the hush of daybreak. "Feeling better?"

He nodded. "Much. Thanks to you."

He watched her eyes, held his breath and waited for the disgust or disappointment he expected. When none was forthcoming, Dax accepted the fact that Jenna Garwood was even more special than he'd originally thought.

"I'm glad."

He held out the mug. "Careful. It's hot."

Expression quizzical, she accepted his offering, wrapping both hands around the cup before sipping daintily. "Thank you."

"Enough cream?"

"Perfect." She started to rise. "I'll finish breakfast now."

The blanket slid away. He replaced it and guided her back down, adding a reassuring squeeze to the delicate bones of her shoulder. "Stay. Weekends are lazy. No rush."

Jenna settled readily and sipped again at the cup. Steam curled upward, wrapping her face in a mist, as if she were a genie who'd appeared to grant his fondest wishes. Ah, if only it were so. But Dax Coleman was the worst kind of realist, a man who barely believed in people, certainly not in pregnant genies. Though if he could believe in anyone, after last night he might believe in Jenna.

Fool that he was.

Turned sideways on the bench, Jenna drew her legs up close to her body and arranged the long ends of a robe and the fleece blanket over them. Her feet peeked out, pink and elegant the way he'd remembered. He hadn't thought about her feet, about those pink-tipped toes, in days. Funny how he wished for an excuse to touch the smooth, soft skin again.

She patted the empty end of the bench. "I'll share my space with you."

Dax hesitated, wondering if spending nonworking time with the housekeeper was a good idea. Considering his fanciful thoughts this morning, it wasn't.

Her mouth curved in a soft smile. "It's so beautiful out here. People should take the time to enjoy these moments."

Hadn't he been thinking the same thing? He eased onto the far end of the bench and leaned forward, letting the coffee cup dangle between his knees. The space between him and Jenna was limited, though, and her toes grazed the side of his thigh. He tried not to think about it but the knowledge that only a layer of denim separated his skin from hers lingered.

"I try to find a few minutes to come out here every morning," she said, her voice soft and dreamy.

He hadn't known that. "No wonder you look tired."

She smiled. "Do I? I'm not really. I'm—" She stopped and sipped at the cup again.

He swiveled his head sideways just enough to watch the thoughts and feelings flit through her eyes. Even in the semilight, her eyes shone with an inner strength and beauty that had him mesmerized. He didn't know when he'd begun thinking of her this way. Maybe he was still asleep with the remnants of the cursed headache impairing his mental function, but the woman was messing with his mind. As hard as he tried to remember she was hardly out of her teens, he failed more often than not.

And last night, she'd offered to undress him.

A white-hot blaze flared in his gut. He tamped it down, glad for the chill morning, though even the fiercest winter wouldn't have cooled the fire Jenna had started inside him.

This morning she was rumpled and uncombed, still in her robe, the likes of which he'd never seen. It was expensive; he knew that much from watching Reba spend like a queen, but even she had never had anything like this. Jenna's urgent need for a job didn't fit with the fancy clothes or the air of upper-crust breeding she wore like a princess. Had her cheating husband left her penniless? Had he taken everything and caused her to run away in shame, destitute?

"You're what?" he asked, picking up the conversation, wanting to know more than he should have, but not willing to ask the questions about her husband. Had she loved him? Did she still?

"Mmm, I don't know how to express it." Her shoulders lifted. "Grateful, I suppose."

He'd wanted her to say happy. How dumb was that? No woman had ever been happy here. Not his mother or his sister or his ex-wife. Too far from the city. Too far from civilization. Too far from friends and shopping malls.

"Different from where you're from, I suspect."

She made a small amused sound. "Oh, yes. Very different."

He couldn't help himself. "Is that a good thing or a bad thing?"

The early-morning quiet, the intimacy of Jenna in her housecoat and blanket, and him remembering the touch of her cool hands against his temples had him talking in ways he wouldn't normally have.

"A very good thing. A person can feel safe here. Free."

He wondered at the assessment, so different from Reba's. She'd felt confined and alone. Jenna felt safe and free. Though he wondered at how such a young woman could know otherwise, another hitch in the terrible knot beneath his heart loosened.

"Wide-open spaces, fresh air, can't beat 'em."

She inhaled deeply. "Just smell that, Dax. So clean and pure." She touched his shirtsleeve. "I smell winter."

Resisting the urge to put his hand over hers, Dax smiled and looked toward the horizon. She had a cute way of putting things.

"You probably smell rain blowing up from the Gulf. Anyway, I hope you do. Lord knows we need it."

"Do we?"

We. He didn't miss the pronoun. "Always need rain out here. That's why we irrigate."

"Ah." She tilted her head in acknowledgment. "What is that sound?"

Dax listened, hearing only the usual noises of a Texas dawn. "Birds, hungry calves bawling for mama."

"No, that other sound. The popping."

His lips curved against the rim of his coffee cup. He'd lived so long with the noises he hardly heard them anymore. "Oil wells some-where. Could be miles away. Out here sound travels forever."

"We don't have those in—back East."

That tiny pause caught in Dax's thoughts. What was it about her past that she wanted to hide? Why didn't she want him to know her hometown?

He mentally rolled his eyes. *Get a clue, Coleman. Women like an escape route.* Last night meant nothing beyond an employee showing kindness. Get over it.

The back door groaned open. Gavin poked his head out. "Dad?"

Both adults turned toward the sound.

"Out here, son."

Dressed in flannel pajamas, his dark hair sticking up in horns all over his head, Gavin stumbled out onto the porch. "What are you doing?"

"Talking. Watching the sunrise."

Gavin's face screwed up tight. "Is it time to get up?"

"Only if you want to."

"Okay." He scratched at his underarm, clearly bewildered by the adults' behavior. "Dad?"

"What?"

"Is your grain better?"

"My what?"

Jenna chuckled softly and touched Dax's arm. They exchanged glances. "My grains. Your grains. Understand?"

The light dawned in Dax's eyes.

"Yes, son," he said. "My headache is gone, thanks to Jenna."

"And me. I was real quiet."

"Yes, you were," Jenna said. "You helped me with Sophie, too."

"Yeah." The dark-haired child stretched, yawning loudly. "It's cold out here. Dad?"

The adults shared another amused glance. "What, son?"

"Can Jenna come to my school again? She wants to, don't you Miss Jenna?"

"Yes, I do, but that's entirely up to your father."

"Why would I care if you went to Gavin's school?"

"They'd like me to volunteer one day a week."

"You want to?"

"Very much, but my first duty is here."

Duty. For some inexplicable reason, the word chafed like starched pants. "Gavin is part of that duty. But you have a life, too, Jenna. You aren't a slave here."

"I know, but I want to do the right thing."

"Volunteer. It will be good for both of you." Good for him, too, not to be thinking about her in his house every minute of the day.

She smiled. "Yes, I believe so, too."

Her smile touched a sore spot inside him. The chafing evaporated. Hadn't he been thinking she needed to get out more?

"This reminds me of something I've been meaning to discuss with you." Since the conversation with Rowdy, the thoughts hadn't let up. Along with a near kiss over a rearranged couch, thinking about her had probably given him the migraine. A woman had needs, even a woman with a new baby. Maybe especially then. He didn't want her getting dissatisfied and running off. Though anyone with half a brain would tell you that Dax Coleman no more knew how to make a woman happy than he could sprout wings and fly. But he had to try.

She was a good cook. Gavin needed her. Things ran smoother since she'd come. He needed to keep her happy.

That gnat of a voice buzzing inside his head said he liked having her around, too, but he swatted it. No use thinking the impossible.

"You want to discuss something?" Jenna tilted her head, one finely shaped eyebrow upraised. "Is it something I'm not doing correctly?"

There were lots of those but he wasn't going there. Who cared about pink socks or a fork down the garbage disposal when she served beef tournedos and salmon roulade—and he wasn't even a fish eater.

"You're doing great," he managed, though complimentary words came out of his throat like opening a rusted door.

That smile came again, tickling his stomach. Dax fidgeted, turning the warm mug in his hands. He wasn't doing this for her smiles. It was self-preservation, plain and simple. He needed a housekeeper who would stick around.

"No woman likes being stuck on a ranch all the time. You need to get out now and then."

Jenna went silent. He shifted a glance in her direction. What he saw troubled him. Gnawing that pretty lip of hers, she looked worried.

What did she have to be worried about?

The notion that she was running from something—or someone—came back to haunt him. He'd vowed to protect her and the little pink princess. He couldn't do much else but he could do that. If someone was after her, they'd have to come through him.

The vehemence of the sentiment stunned him.

"I just mean—" What did he mean? Rowdy said women needed to go out and have fun. If he wanted to keep her happily employed, he'd have to make that happen. Though not with Rowdy.

"I thought we might go to a movie," he blurted.

"Dinner, too, if you want." He couldn't believe he'd said that.

"You want to take me to a movie?" she asked.

Dax swallowed. Could he handle spending more time with a woman who was already messing with his head? And exactly when had he starting thinking of her as a woman?

"I don't want you to feel trapped here. A night out is good for you now and then. I don't want to put any pressure on you, either. I mean, you're my employee so if you don't want to go, that's fine. Just feel free to go out on your own or with someone else any time you feel like it. Don't let the job stop you. That's what I meant." The last statements ground against him like a handful of rocks in his boot. He didn't want her going out with anyone. "Not one of the hands, though. These cowboys. You can't trust them." He was babbling.

Jenna looked at him as if the headache had caused more mental stress than she'd originally thought. Maybe it had.

Gavin, on the other hand, had come to life. With enough glee to start his own clown act, he began hopping up and down on one foot, slapping his arms. "Say yes, Miss Jenna. Dad will even spring for a Friendly Meal. Won't you, Dad?"

"Oh, Gavin, you charmer." Jenna pressed a hand to her lips and laughed.

Dax's shoulders relaxed. He grinned. "Yeah, I'm a big spender."

Jenna's amused gaze captured Dax's. "Then I shall be delighted to accept your kind invitation. A movie and a Friendly Meal it shall be."

No matter how hard he tried to convince himself he was doing this to keep her happy as well as safely away from Rowdy, Dax realized one thing. He was in big trouble.

CHAPTER ELEVEN

A MOVIE. DAX WAS TAKING her to a movie.

Jenna couldn't keep the smile off her face as she dressed that evening. What did one wear to a movie?

She opened the closet and browsed, regretting the decision to leave her dress clothes behind. The only public movie she'd ever attended was a premiere in New York. Derek had insisted on going, and later she'd realized he was enamored of the starlet who had invited them. She had deplored the ostentatious glitz and posturing, preferring the privacy of their home theater.

A regular movie outing would likely be different. Most people—*normal* people—did not wear Versace gowns to a movie.

Which was fine with Jenna. She'd left the gowns behind with the rest of her life. From her knowledge of the people of Saddleback, she was certain a movie was not a black-tie affair.

The hangers scraped over the metal bar as she sorted through the clothes she'd brought with her. Up to now she'd mostly worn her loose-fitting maternity outfits, but with her tummy regaining shape, she took out a pair of jeans, a long-sleeved top and a pink leather jacket. They weren't Western wear by any stretch of the imagination, but they would do.

She slithered into the jeans, a snug fit, and spritzed eau de parfum in all the right places before sliding the blouse over her head. In front of the mirror, she turned this way and that, casting a critical eye on her appearance. She might not be beautiful, but she knew how to put herself together for the best effect. A Carrington always kept up appearances.

Her hair had lost its trendy cut, but a few minutes with a straightener and some shine serum made it presentable. Humming, she slipped on jewelry and heels, then went to dress the baby for their first night out in Saddleback, Texas.

By the time she entered the living room to await the men of the group, her palms were damp with excitement.

Gavin appeared first, strutting through the

house with his chest puffed out, his black-brown hair slicked down and dressed in perfectly creased jeans and a red button-down shirt. His boots gleamed with a fresh polish.

"My goodness. You look immaculate."

"Yeah," he said proudly, craning his neck to one side. "Smell me." He pointed to a spot on his neck. "Right there. Daddy put me on some of his smell-good."

With an inward smile, Jenna inhaled loudly. "Wonderful."

If Dax smelled this delicious, she might swoon.

The man in question ambled down the hall into sight. Jenna's heart banged once hard against her rib cage. He was definitely swoonworthy.

"Everyone ready?"

"Yearning for that Friendly Meal," she joked.

"Yeah," Gavin sighed. "I love Friendly Meals."

The adults exchanged glances. For a nano-second their gazes locked and a feeling of pure pleasure danced between them.

"No headache?" she asked.

He touched his temple. "Good as new."

She reached for Sophie's carrier, but Dax nudged her out of the way. "I've got the princess. You grab the diaper bag."

She did as he said, covertly watching her employer tap the baby's nose and make faces at her. Sophie, her usual drowsy self, let her eyes cross and then closed them as Dax draped a blanket over the entire baby seat.

Feeling happy in a way she had never dreamed possible, Jenna walked alongside Dax and Gavin out the door and to his truck.

She helped Dax position the car seat in the back with Gavin and smiled her thanks when he helped her into the cab, closed the door and grinned at her through the glass before jogging around to the driver's side.

Yes, indeed, being a normal, everyday woman was beginning to feel very, very good.

Dax sat across the orange plastic table from Jenna watching her and Gavin devour French fries with the same zeal. He'd tried to take them someplace nicer, but she'd insisted on the burger joint. He was sure she'd done so for Gavin's sake and he appreciated that, but she deserved a classier establishment.

Part of him wanted to be sorry he'd asked her out, but tonight he just wanted to laugh and have a good time. When was the last time he'd done that? He didn't even know. From the looks of Gavin, hanging upside down inside the indoor playland, he felt the same. His squeals of laughter mingled with those of a dozen other kids out for a good time on Saturday night.

Dax looked around the colorful dining area, raising a hand to acknowledge a person here and there. He knew most people in Saddleback but hadn't seen them all that much during the last few years. It struck him that the world was moving right along without him to the detriment of his son.

Reba had driven him into a shell. Jenna was bringing him out.

"You have ketchup on your face," he said, pointing.

She took a paper napkin and swiped. "Did I get it?"

"Here." He leaned across the table, took the napkin and cleaned away the drop on her upper lip. "Messy."

The smell of her perfume had driven him batty in the truck, and now he smelled those flowers again. He sat back but the scent lingered in his nostrils.

"You look pretty tonight," he said and then wanted to jam a handful of fries down his throat and strangle himself. He'd brought her out as a means of keeping her employed, not to admire how good she looked in those jeans and that pricey-looking jacket.

Right, and all his cows would jump over the moon at midnight.

Her smile took away the urge to hurt himself. "Thank you. I wasn't sure what to wear."

Women. From the curve of golden hair against her slim face to the silver dangling from her wrist and ears, Jenna was a knockout. "You look great. Perfect." Shut up, Dax.

A hint of pink crested her cheekbones. "What time does the movie start?"

Relieved at the change of subjects, he checked his watch. "Soon. We'd better round up the boy and head that way."

Jenna nodded and began piling discarded wrappers and cups onto the plastic tray before following him to the yellow-and-red tube slide.

"Gavin, come on, son. Time to go."

"He's having such fun."

"Yeah. I liked this stuff when I was a kid, too." An odd look crossed her face. "Didn't you?"

She shook her head. "I've never played on one."

As if she'd said something wrong, she turned

away to fiddle with Sophie. Dax studied her, baffled. She'd never played on a playground?

"Why not?"

"Oh, it's not important. Look, here's Gavin," she said a little too brightly as if they hadn't just seen the boy moments ago when he was dancing in ecstasy over a Friendly Meal toy.

Whatever troubled Jenna about the past, she didn't want to talk about it. Dax decided to let the moment slide. He'd suggested this outing for her pleasure and he wasn't about to mess things up if he could help it. But one of these days Miss Jenna was going to talk to him.

One of these days.

The drive to the movie was a matter of blocks. Once inside the small theater, Dax paid for the tickets. The smell of popcorn enticed Gavin, so they stopped at the concession stand, as well. Cheesy-looking Christmas garland looped from the ceiling, and the walls were plastered with colorful posters of upcoming holiday movies. A cheap, fake Christmas tree stood in one corner of the lobby, lights blinking in lazy cheer. Dax would swear it was the same tree from six or seven years ago.

Jenna stared around with a half smile as if

thrilled with the decor. While he waited for the slowest clerk in Texas to fill his order, Jenna gazed around, watching the good folks of Saddleback mingle and talk.

Teenagers swarmed the lobby, holding hands and talking too loud over the video games. Dax thought of how Jenna belonged more with them than with him. Though he felt a little better to see she had a serene maturity they all lacked.

He watched her soaking it all in, an enchanted expression on her face, as if attending a two-screen theater in a tiny town was the coolest thing ever. That was Jenna. She had a way of making a celebration out of everyday life.

The clerk finally brought their order.

"Ready?" he said to Jenna.

She nodded, the light of excitement in her eyes almost too much to believe.

Balancing popcorn and sodas along with Sophie and her gear, they wandered down the semilit aisle to a row of seats.

Jostling elbows and baby carrier, they settled in and the movie started. The loud music startled Sophie who began to whimper. Jenna removed her from the carrier and rocked her back and forth until she settled. The baby scent mingled with popcorn and the distinctive smell of a movie theater. Dax kicked back and relaxed with his snacks. Might as well enjoy himself.

The animated Christmas film had Gavin giggling from the get-go. Thirty minutes in, though, he had to go to the bathroom. When they returned, Sophie was fussing again and Jenna grappled in the dark for a bottle from the diaper bag.

Without giving the action much thought, Dax took the baby while Jenna found the bottle. When she reached for Sophie, he shook his head, taking the bottle from her.

"I got her," he whispered.

Jenna looked more grateful than he'd expected. His conscience tweaked. He'd wanted her to relax and have a good time, but here she was wrestling the fussy baby.

He slipped the bottle into Sophie's mouth. She latched on like a baby 'possum.

Maybe he should have gotten a babysitter, but he'd never hired a sitter and didn't know where to start. Besides, the children made for a good buffer, so the night out didn't feel like a date. It was more like a family outing.

The notion stuck in the center of his brain and wouldn't move until he examined it. Family. This was what he'd always wanted, the thing that was missing in his life, and tonight he felt as if he and Jenna and Gavin and Sophie belonged together.

He squirmed in the chair and tried to concentrate on the pink princess staring up at him as if he was some kind of hero.

When at last Sophie slept again, he handed her over to Jenna who in turn placed her in the carrier.

"Thank you," she whispered, leaning toward his ear. Her arm bumped his from shoulder to elbow. In the flickering light of animation, he saw her smile.

His stomach went airborne.

He reached for her hand and she gave it willingly.

He swallowed hard, pretended to watch the dancing elves and ignored the warning bells going off in his head.

It was only a movie, only a hand. Just that sentimental Christmasy feeling. No big deal.

Tomorrow things would return to normal.

The night air was crisp and quiet when the moviegoers returned to the Southpaw. A banana moon tilted overhead as though paying homage to the stunning spray of stars in the indigo sky.

Careful to cover her daughter against the

chilled air, Jenna made her way to the door. Dax strode alongside with a sleeping Gavin slung over one shoulder.

She had never dreamed a night at a fast-food restaurant and a run-down movie theater could be such pleasure. She cast a sidelong glance at her companion. Dax was the main cause of her enjoyment. At the restaurant, he'd teased her about the amount of ketchup she'd dumped on her French fries and told her funny stories about his first few months of taking care of a newborn. Between the lines, she'd read the desperation and sorrow he must have felt. Knowing his struggle matched her own had made his humor all the more endearing.

Then they'd laughed at the funny Christmas movie, and he'd held her hand, such a simple thing, but her entire body had hummed in pleasure. She wondered what it would be like to go on a real date with him, a dangerous thought perhaps, given who she was and the things she'd kept from him. But just this once she wanted someone—a male someone—to see her as something besides a trust fund.

Everything with Derek had been a secret until after their elopement. Secret meetings and stolen kisses in the university library had meant nothing to him but money.

Dax shifted Gavin's lax body, holding on to the child with one strong arm while he maneuvered the house key and opened the door.

"Youth and beauty before age and treachery," he teased, voice quiet.

He stood to the side, holding the door with his back while she passed through with the baby. She recalled that first day when Rowdy had crowded her in the doorway and she'd been repelled. Not so with Dax. He could stand as close as he wanted.

Of course, he didn't. He padded down the hall with the sleeping Gavin while she headed in the opposite direction to change and settle Sophie for the night, chastising herself for trying to make something significant from the evening. Dax was being kind, asking her to join in an outing with his son. That's all there was to it.

Sophie was sound asleep, rousing only slightly as Jenna changed and swaddled her for the night. After snapping on the elephant night-light, Jenna returned to the living room, hoping for an opportunity to let Dax know how much she'd enjoyed the night out.

She wasn't disappointed. Dax came down the

hall toward her, rubbing the back of his neck. When
he saw her standing there, he offered a crooked
grin. "That boy could sleep through a tornado."

She answered with a smile. "He had fun tonight."

"Yeah. We haven't done that much." He plopped
down on the couch. "I like this new arrangement."

The comment brought back the memory of that
day when she'd thought he might kiss her.

"Why?"

"Because it looks nice," he said.

"No, I mean why haven't you and Gavin gone
out much?"

"Oh. Good question. I don't know."

She smiled and settled on the end of the sofa,
wanting to sit near again but unsure if he wanted
that. "Would you like something to eat or drink?"

He looked horrified. "Are you kidding?"

"Yes. Nothing like a Friendly Meal and popcorn
to fill me up."

"Sorry about that. Next time—"

He stopped but Jenna caught on the phrase. Was
he thinking about a next time?

"I'm serious. I loved the Friendly Meal."

He looked dubious, but said, "For a skinny girl
you can put away the fries."

"I just had a baby. I am not skinny."

His gaze roved lazily over her, not in an insolent way as Rowdy's had done, but with an appreciation that made her knees wobble.

"I had a good time," he said softly, capturing her eyes with his.

"Thank you for asking me. The evening was wonderful."

"Are you happy here, Jenna?"

What a strange question. "Happier than I've ever been in my life."

The admission came as naturally as breathing. She was happy here, living a dream, bringing her daughter up the way she'd wanted to be. Safe and free and normal.

Dax's nostrils flared.

Everything in her longed to travel the short distance down the couch to him. The memory of his almost kiss stayed with her and she saw it now reflected in his eyes.

"Jenna?" The whisker-rough voice sent tingles down her spine.

"Yes?" she whispered.

A beat of silence quivered in the air before Dax dragged a hand over his face and looked away. "I guess we should call it a night."

Jenna wilted with disappointed. When he said

nothing else, only stared at the cold fireplace, Jenna rose. "Then I shall bid you good-night."

Stiffly, she left the room, not daring to look back, lest he see the longing in her face and pity her. Or worse yet, dismiss her. She'd misinterpreted his kindness, for that's all this lovely night had been.

CHAPTER TWELVE

AT HIGH NOON the next Thursday, the tables at Lydia's Lunchbox were jammed with diners. Jenna stood in the crowded entry, soaking up the sights and sounds—the clink of plates and forks, the soft laughter and conversation, the drawling accents she found so entertaining. In the back corner, she spotted a hand waving at her.

"Over here, Jenna." Crystal Wolf had become the kind of friend she'd always wanted.

"This place is really crowded today," she said as she settled into a chair.

"Lydia's is the best place in town for a light lunch. Besides, Pam's Diner is closed until after the first of the year." Crystal peeled the blanket off Sophie. "I swear, hon, she gets prettier every time I see her."

Pride swelled inside Jenna. Her little girl *was* beautiful and she looked adorable today in her hot pink mouse cap with matching jumper and shoes. "Her pointed head went away just as you predicted."

Crystal laughed. "Of course. I didn't go to nursing school for nothing. You look great, too. Wow." The other woman looked her over. "What is going on with you? You look…radiant. If having a baby makes a woman look that good, I need to have five or six."

Crystal and her husband had been married for several years but hadn't started a family.

Jenna shook out a napkin and placed it on her lap. "You saw me at my very worst in the hospital. Anything has to be an improvement on that."

"Sure, but you look different today."

"Same old me," she said, although she wondered if that was exactly the truth. Since the night out with Dax, she'd felt buoyant, excited as though something new and wonderful was just around the corner. "Must be the Christmas spirit. I'm having such fun decorating the house."

The waitress arrived and took their orders. Jenna could care less what she ate. She was delighted with the new freedom to make her own friends and go where she wanted.

Crystal patted Sophie before taking up her own napkin. "Any more domestic disasters?"

Jenna laughed. She'd told her friend about the pink socks and flooded kitchen. "Let's just say learning to be a good housekeeper is an even sharper learning curve than caring for a newborn. If Dax weren't so sweet, he would have fired me the second day."

The waitress appeared with their order of chicken salad sandwiches and veggie slices. Crystal's hand paused over the julienne carrots. "Sweet? Did you just refer to Dax as sweet?"

"Well, maybe *sweet* isn't the right word." Jenna was positive her cheeks flamed. She reached for her glass of water. "He's been very supportive and kind."

"Mmm, I see." The woman's gaze was speculative. "Looks good, too, doesn't he?"

"I'd be lying if I said no. But Dax is more than good-looking, Crystal. He's such a man, so protective and helpful." She refrained from adding that she felt safe with Dax in a way she'd seldom experienced in her childhood or her marriage. Crystal didn't know about her past. "Do you know he wouldn't allow me to move the furniture? He was afraid I'd hurt myself."

"This is getting more interesting by the minute." Jenna reached for another cucumber slice.

"You once told me that Dax Coleman was one of the good guys. You were right. Going into labor in this town was the best thing that ever happened to me. I love my job. The ranch is beautiful. Dax's little boy is a treasure. I'm even volunteering at the school every Tuesday and I'm planning a Christmas party. You're invited, of course."

"Dax is having a Christmas party?"

"Let's just say he has tentatively agreed to this whing-ding, as he calls it." She scrunched her shoulders in excitement. "It will be so much fun, and Dax could use a bit of Christmas cheer."

"There's no doubting that." Crystal stirred her cup of herbal tea and laid the spoon carefully aside. "I'm very impressed by the way you've assimilated, Jenna. When I first met you, I wasn't sure how you'd cope."

Necessity was a fast teacher. "I love it here," she said, drawing in a deep, contented breath. "I'm happier than I've ever been in my life."

Jenna hadn't meant to add the last line but her friend already knew she'd suffered heartache. She just didn't know the real reasons.

"You look happy. You sound happy." Crystal studied her over a bite of chicken salad. "That's it. That's the difference I see in you today. You're in love with Dax."

Jenna nearly choked on a drink of water. She clunked the glass onto the tabletop and stared at Crystal. Blood rushed through her head like a hard rain.

"In love?" she croaked.

Crystal tilted her head. White earrings flashed against her dark skin. "Aren't you?"

"I—" Jenna blinked. Once. Twice. She lifted a hand to her mouth. "Oh dear."

"Honey!" A warm hand closed over Jenna's arm and gave it a shake. "That's fantastic. I'm so happy for you."

"No. I don't know." She floundered. "Dax doesn't…"

"Dax doesn't what? Know you've fallen for him? Or return the feelings?"

"Both." She gripped her friend's fingers. "Promise you won't say a word."

"My lips are sealed. But let me tell you, hon, Dax Coleman is carrying a load of hurt. He may take some time and effort, but I know one thing, when that man falls, he falls hard."

Yes, Dax was the kind of man who would keep a commitment. Hadn't she seen that in the way he'd wanted to be certain she and Sophie were safe and well after the unexpected birth? Maybe that's why he'd never recovered from the divorce. "Do you know what happened with his wife?"

Crystal's long hair fell forward as she nodded. "Everyone in Saddleback knows. She left him for another man."

"After Gavin was born."

"Yes, and to make things worse, the man she ran off with was Sam Coleman, Dax's younger brother."

Jenna's stomach dropped to her shoes. "Oh no. Poor Dax."

"Some thought Reba suffered from post-partum depression, but I never believed that. She was always wild and needed constant male attention. Sam wasn't her first lover. She'd been cheating on Dax for a long time. I guess everyone knew but him."

No wonder Dax had become so reclusive. He'd been as humiliated by Reba as Jenna had been by Derek. More so. Both his spouse and his brother had betrayed him.

Jenna's conscience tugged. Wasn't it betrayal of a different kind not to tell him about her trust fund?

She fought off the worry, convinced she and

Sophie were safe as long as no one knew who they were. Not even Dax.

She and Crystal went on talking, jumping from subject to subject. Crystal was a wealth of information about babies and housekeeping, Dax and the people of Saddleback, and the best places for Christmas shopping. Gaining this woman as a friend had been nothing short of a pre-Christmas miracle.

Finally, Jenna glanced at her watch. Gavin would be home soon, so the women reluctantly parted ways with the promise to meet again the following week.

All the way back to the Southpaw, Jenna mulled over the personal revelations that had come out over a chicken salad sandwich. She was falling in love with her employer, her rescuer, a man with deep emotional wounds. Gavin, though he'd never known Reba, was wounded, too. He sensed his father's pain and overprotection. The insecurity had given rise to an inner fear and a timid nature. Jenna didn't know how she understood this, but she did.

Maybe love gave a woman insight.

Casting a glance at Sophie in the rearview

mirror, she smiled at the thought. What she'd had with Derek could never compare to this. She was almost ashamed to admit that Derek had been an escape route, a means to escape the prison of her life under Elaine Carrington's paranoid eye. What she felt for Dax and Gavin went deeper— all the way to the center of her heart.

The troubling conscience pressed in again. If she loved Dax, didn't he deserve to know the truth about her situation?

She bit down on her bottom lip, gnawing the skin in the same way the question gnawed away at her heart. Maybe she should tell him.

But what if she was being a fool again? What if her emotions clouded her reason? She'd thought she was in love before and look what had happened.

But this was different. Dax was different. She was different.

But Dax was not in love with her. He didn't even find her attractive enough to kiss, a fact that had been painfully clear the night of the Christmas movie. He was good to her and Sophie, but kindness did not translate into love. Her nanny was kind. Her bodyguards were kind.

She was an employee just as they had been.

By the time she had taken Sophie into the house and had returned for the shopping bags, she was convinced that keeping quiet was the best thing to do. Any decision she made affected her daughter, and Sophie's life would not be a repeat of hers. Until she could win love on her own terms, without the lure of the Carrington fortune, Jenna would keep her secret.

Bending, she reached into the backseat for the bags. The cold wind swept through the car, beneath her jacket and made her shiver. Paper and plastic crinkled as she hurried, eager to get inside the warm house. A masculine arm snaked from behind her and latched onto a bag. Her heart reacted happily. Dax must have seen her struggling in the wind and come to assist.

She spun around, smile ready. "Dax," she started but then the pleasure drained from her.

Rowdy stood, trapping her between the car door and the backseat, a grocery bag in hand.

"Sorry, darlin', if you were expecting the boss. It's just faithful Rowdy coming to your rescue. You don't mind some help with these bags, do you?"

Jenna swallowed back her disappointment and misgivings. "Thank you. I can manage."

She bent for another bag before realizing that Rowdy was probably staring at her backside.

"Old Dax would have my hide if I let a lady handle this alone. It's cold out here." He stood too close, that insufferable grin taunting her.

Jenna sighed and tightened her jaw. She was not going to let this guy get under her skin. "As you wish, then. I'll offer my thanks if you will please be so kind as to get out of my way. My daughter is already in the house and I don't like to leave her alone."

"Yes, ma'am," he said, though his tone mocked her as he backed off. "Lead the way. I'll bring the rest."

Aware of his eyes on her, Jenna hurried inside. Perhaps she was overreacting. Perhaps the cowboy was genuine in his offer of help. But he gave her the creeps.

Rowdy followed her into the house and though she would have preferred he leave immediately, she didn't want to be rude. She began putting the groceries in the cabinets.

"You wouldn't happen to have a cold drink for a hot man, would you?"

Jenna ignored the double entendre. There was no way he had worked up a sweat in this weather.

She took a can of orange soda from the refrigerator, handed it to him and went back to work. Rowdy leaned an elbow against the granite countertop and watched her.

"I've been meaning to ask you something, Jenna."

She slid a carton of eggs onto the refrigerator rack and shut the door. Cool air wafted out. "What is it?"

"A friend of mine is having a party Saturday night. I thought you might want to get out of here, have some fun."

"Thank you for the kind offer but I have a baby."

"So we hire a sitter. I know lots of girls."

She imagined he did. "I really can't."

"Ah, come on. We'll have fun."

"I—I already have plans." It was a lie worth telling.

"Cancel them."

The man wouldn't take no for an answer.

"I'd prefer not to." She started around him.

He grabbed her elbow. His face hardened. "So what's the deal? You and Dax have something going? Is that why you won't go out with me?"

She stiffened. "I beg your pardon?"

He laughed, though the sound didn't delight.

"You sure are cute when you talk prissy. Come on, Jenna, throw me a bone. I'll show you a good time."

She tugged her arm, but his fingers bit into the flesh. "Please let me go."

"On one condition."

She sighed. "I really can't go out with you. Please. I have duties here."

"What kind of duties, Jenna?" He yanked at her, pulling her so close she could smell his breath. He'd been drinking. "What exactly does Dax pay you for?"

She went as cold as ice inside. "I do not appreciate the insinuation. Please unhand me."

"Sure thing, darlin'." He pulled her closer. "Just one little kiss and I'll be on my way."

"I don't think so."

"Well, think again, honey." And his face descended.

Dax wiped his boots on the mat, eager to get inside and tell Jenna the news. That mare she liked was going to foal tonight. But first he took extra care not to track unmentionable stuff onto the clean carpet and tile. She never complained, but she'd given him the evil eye a couple of times. He did not want to make his housekeeper unhappy.

Shaking his head, he chuckled to himself. Fancy-talking Jenna with her real fur house shoes and gourmet meals was quickly becoming more than a housekeeper. She was becoming a part of his life and of Gavin's. The Christmas decor that looked like something out of a magazine wasn't the only thing full of cheer in this once-somber ranch house.

As he crossed the foyer and living room, he heard her voice. She was probably on the phone inviting someone else to the Christmas whing-ding. His smile widened. She even had him looking forward to the invasion of his privacy.

Her tone rose higher. Another voice answered. A male voice. Stomach dropping like a brick, Dax stopped to listen. What was a man doing in the kitchen with Jenna?

A flash of memory made him shudder. Reba, half-naked, in the arms of his brother.

He bit down on his back teeth and shook away the image. Jenna was not his cheating, lying wife.

Yet the dread weighing him down wouldn't go away. He started forward then stopped again to listen.

The pair in the kitchen were not murmuring love words. Jenna's voice sounded strained, frightened. Tension hummed in the air.

Adrenaline kicked in. Something was wrong.

He rounded the wall into the kitchen. His first vision was of Rowdy and Jenna, bodies pressed close. Their mouths were mere inches apart.

The memory of Reba in Sam's arms came again. Pain slammed through Dax, stealing his breath.

Stuck between Rowdy and the counter, Jenna twisted her face to one side. "Stop it, Rowdy. Stop it."

One hand came up to press at Rowdy's chest.

Dax shook his head, battling down the past to understand the present.

Jenna was not inviting Rowdy's attentions. On the contrary. She was resisting.

Relief replaced jealousy. Just as quickly a cold fury washed over him.

Fist clenched, he stormed into the kitchen. "You heard the lady, Davis. Back off."

Rowdy's grip loosened. Jenna jerked to one side, face flaming. She rubbed at her arm. Dax's fury turned white-hot. If she was hurt…

"Hey, boss." Rowdy turned slowly and raised

both hands like a criminal. "Everything's cool here. No harm done."

"Doesn't look that way to me." Dax opened his fist, clenched it again. He was half an inch from punching out his best cowboy. He flicked a glance at Jenna. "You okay?"

Still rubbing her arm, face the color of paste, she nodded. The anxiety radiating off her made him even angrier. Rowdy Davis might be a good hand, but he had no business coming into the house to harass Jenna.

Rowdy shifted backward one step, his eyes never leaving Dax's face. "I'll just be heading back to the barn then."

Dax wagged his head. "I don't think so. You're done here. For good."

Rowdy's mouth dropped. "You're not letting me go because of her, are you?"

"Yeah, I am. Get out, Rowdy, before I lose my temper."

The cowboy's mouth curled in a sneer. "Don't be stupid, Coleman. I'm the best manager around."

Dax was afraid his jaw was going to snap. "We don't need your kind here."

"What about her kind? What's the deal, boss?

Why are you so jumpy about an unwed house-keeper with a brat in tow?"

Jenna's gasp drew Dax's gaze. If possible, she'd grown whiter. She pressed a shocked hand to her lips.

"She's a widow."

Rowdy laughed, an ugly sound. "Yeah, and I'm Santa Claus. Ho-ho-*ho*." The last syllable was aimed maliciously at Jenna.

Dax's restraint snapped. He drew back a fist. Before he could throw the punch, a soft hand caught his.

"Please, Dax. No."

Dax turned, incredulous. "You're defending him?"

"No. I just want him to leave me alone." Her voice quivered. "Gavin will be here soon. I don't want him to witness fisticuffs."

Jenna's concern was for Gavin, not for herself. The anger toward Rowdy increased until Dax trembled with the need for a physical release.

"Get your gear and get off my property, Davis, before I satisfy a powerful hankering to break your nose."

Rowdy postured for a few seconds, weighing his options. Apparently, he was smart enough to know when he'd lost. With a curse that Dax hadn't allowed past his own lips in years, the fired cowboy slammed out of the house.

He'd no more than cleared the room when Dax turned to Jenna. "How are you really? And don't say okay."

As she opened her mouth to reply, her lips trembled. That was his undoing. He folded her into his arms. She nestled against him, her soft breath puffing warm against his neck. Her body quivered.

So did his.

He stroked her back and murmured as he'd done the day she'd given birth. The reminder of that shared intimacy swirled inside him, provocative in a way that shook him to his boot heels. He recalled her strength and grit, her frantic concern for her infant. He recalled the way she'd looked at him as though he was the greatest hero ever.

With an inner groan, Dax squeezed his eyes shut.

A hero. He wanted to be a hero. Her hero.

He was a fool. A woman his own age had dumped him. What made him think Jenna, a woman years younger and with far more inner beauty and refinement, would think of him as anything but a worn-out old cowboy?

Yet, he went on holding her against his chest,

feeling the thud of her heart so close to his that the rhythms seemed to be one.

A tangle of thoughts coursed through his head.

He wasn't falling for her. No way. It was inappropriate. She was his employee, a young mother, a *very* young mother. She thought of him as a protector, a friend, maybe even an uncle.

Yeah, that was it. An uncle.

"Dax?" Jenna murmured.

He smoothed a hand down the back of her head, over the soft hair, and filled his nostrils with her orange blossom fragrance.

He cleared his throat, thick with some troubling emotion. "Yeah?"

Jenna lifted her head from his chest and tilted her face up to look at him. "Thank you."

Her lips curved, drawing his attention.

He couldn't keep his eyes from a glance at her mouth. He'd thought about it, maybe even dreamed about it.

"Ah, Jenna."

She placed a hand against his cheek, the curved smile deepening. "My hero," she whispered. "Again."

With warning bells clanging like fire engines, Dax groaned, aware he should walk away now while he still could. He started to loosen his hold but Jenna held tight.

"Kiss me this time, Dax. Please." She tiptoed up, waiting.

The request was his undoing.

Just once, he told himself. Just this one time.

With his heart pounding in both fear and hope, Dax cupped her face and pressed his lips to hers.

CHAPTER THIRTEEN

JENNA TUCKED A BLANKET around the sleeping Sophie, kissed her velvet cheek and snapped off the overhead light, though she remained in the semidarkness gazing at her daughter while she thought about the eventful day.

The scene with Rowdy had both embarrassed and unnerved her, but Dax's reaction had shaken her to the core. She still couldn't believe he'd fired his ranch manager because of her. More than that, she couldn't believe he'd finally kissed her. Kissed her in a way she'd never been kissed. Tender and ravenous and with such care, as if she were fragile crystal in danger of shattering.

She'd wanted him never to stop, but they'd both heard the front door open and the sound of Gavin's book bag thump onto the coffee table. With a wry twist of that delicious mouth, Dax had pressed his forehead to hers, given her a look that would melt steel, then gone to greet his son.

Jenna touched a finger to her lips, feeling him there even now and foolishly wishing to repeat the pleasure. Dax Coleman, with only the touch of his mouth, had given hope to an impossible dream.

At dinner he'd been unusually quiet and thoughtful and Jenna wondered what he was thinking. Dare she dream that he was as stunned as she? For stunned she was. Stunned by the emotions roaring through her. Stunned to feel so complete in his arms. Stunned to be falling in love.

Could Dax possibly feel the same? Or was he instead filled with regret about a rash behavior?

All through the meal of beef medallions and pasta, he'd said little and afterward had left the house, using the excuse of a mare about to give birth. She'd wanted to go out to the barn with him to watch the miracle, but he hadn't asked and she didn't quite have the courage to impose.

Perhaps they both needed time to process what had happened. Her optimistic side believed he felt something special for her. He was certainly a better, braver, stronger man than Derek, but it was Derek's betrayal that kept her afraid.

Sensitive Gavin must have felt the tension

between the adults because he'd been clingy and whiny all evening. She'd made a special effort to focus on him, finally bringing out the ingredients for baked dough ornaments. Working the dough with his hands and cutting the shapes seemed to ease his stress and by storytime Gavin seemed happier.

Still, when she'd put him to bed, he'd hugged her a long, heart-tugging time. After she flipped off the light and stepped into the hall, he'd called out, "Jenna."

Expecting a request for a drink, she'd said, "Yes, Gavin."

"I love you."

A perfect peace settled in her soul.

She loved him, too. She'd loved him since the first time she'd found him standing guard over Sophie's crib. With every day that passed, she loved him more.

With an ache for the little boy's hungry heart, she'd gone back into the darkened room for another hug. "I love you, too, Gavin." She'd kissed his forehead. "You're a very special boy."

Now, restless and too keyed-up to sleep, she padded down the hall toward the living room. The house still smelled warm and delicious from the cinnamon in the dough ornaments. Tomorrow they would be cool enough to paint and string with red ribbon for hanging on the tree.

The prelit, flocked spruce Dax had brought from a storage room filled a corner of the dark living room. She plugged in the lights, basking in the beauty she and the Coleman males had created. A lighted wreath sprigged with holly, along with swags of plush, snow-doused garland hung over the fireplace. More garland, flocked and sprinkled with tiny white lights, draped around fat red candles and down the sides of the mantel. Soon the stockings she'd been personalizing would be ready to hang.

At her parents' estate, she'd never been allowed to participate in Christmas preparations other than shopping. A designer had always been retained for the occasion. But Jenna had watched and longed for the day she could create a Christmas of the heart with her own special touches.

Touching a shiny red ball with one fingertip, she smiled softly. That day had finally come in a most unexpected manner and in an even more unexpected place.

She heard Gavin stir and tiptoed down the long hall to his room. He tossed restlessly and murmured, then settled again. She waited a moment longer before returning to the living room, where she went to the window and gazed out. A heavy frost lay over the brown grass and glistened beneath the moon. A Texas night could be so still, and yet she knew life teemed all around her.

The quiet snick of the door latch turned her around. Dax, shoulders hunched against the cold, came inside, filling up the room and her heart. Her stomach fluttered, foolishly happy. One kiss shouldn't mean so much, but to her, it did.

"Hey," he said softly.

"Hey." She'd never said *hey* to anyone in her life, but it sounded right in this place and time. Voice as quiet as his, she went on, "How's the mare?"

"Getting close. I thought you might like to be there."

The foolish happiness expanded. "I was hoping you'd ask."

He tilted his head, serious green eyes reflecting the spare light from the Christmas tree. "Were you?"

She nodded, staying still, not wanting to move away from the way he was looking at her. "Yes."

He breathed in through his nose and exhaled. "Smells good in here."

"Gavin and I made ornament cookies. With cinnamon."

"Bet he liked that."

"I think so."

"You've been good for him."

Jenna's mind stumbled on the past tense. Was he going to let her go? Or had the turn of phrase been unintentional?

The balloon of happiness deflated but filled again when Dax motioned toward her end of the house. "Get your coat. It's cold out."

"Don't you want something hot to drink first?"

"Later. The barn is warm enough, and as you know, babies don't wait." His face lightened at the reminder of Sophie's untimely birth.

She laughed softly. "No, they don't."

Feeling both unsettled and excited, Jenna hurried to her closet for coat and gloves, glanced in on Sophie, then slid the baby monitor into her pocket before returning to Dax.

He was in the kitchen, eyeing the pans of cookie ornaments with an unreadable expression. When he felt her approach, he said, "Ready?"

She nodded and they headed outside and across the glistening yard. The air was every bit as crisp and cold as the frost implied.

Dax took her elbow and guided them through the darkness toward a long, lighted horse barn. Neither spoke, and the only sounds were their soft footsteps and the pounding of her pulse against her eardrums. His touch, his nearness set her entire body a-hum.

She shivered once but otherwise ignored the cold. She felt invigorated, alive, her blood pumping through her veins with new strength and clarity. She was in love with Dax Coleman. In love.

She glanced his way. His face was in shadow but the shape was strong and masculine. She felt comforted and safe in this foreign world of rural Texas with Dax at her side.

Did he know what he had done to her? Did he have any idea how much he'd helped her grow and mature? She'd run away from Pennsylvania a scared girl. Today she was a woman.

He felt something for her, she was certain. But what? Gratitude? Responsibility? Did she dare to believe a man as handsome and honorable as Dax could really find her attractive?

"She's in the third stall," Dax said as he released her elbow to slide back the enormous metal door.

Jenna blinked against the bright, overhead light. The barn, surprisingly warm, smelled clean and grassy with the overtone of warm animals. She liked this barn just as she liked the big, soft-eyed horses who resided here. When time permitted, she brought Gavin inside to pet the horses, hoping that exposure would lessen his fears.

She followed Dax inside stall number three, standing just inside while he approached the mother-to-be. Blanca, as white as her name implied, lay on clean straw with her back legs folded beneath her. Her massive chest rose and fell with the effort of labor. Jenna empathized.

"How ya doin', Blanca girl?" Dax asked as he knelt beside the mare and ran a hand over her glossy hip. He tossed a glance toward Jenna. "Ease on over here. She won't mind."

Jenna did as he instructed, crouching next to him.

"Look right there," he murmured.

Jenna's stomach leaped. She grasped the thick quilting of Dax's sleeve. "Is that the baby?"

"Yep. In good position, too, nose and knees first. We should have touchdown any minute now." There was excitement in his voice that matched the rising tide of energy inside her.

"I've never seen an animal born."

His mouth curved. "First time for everything. I'd never seen a baby born before Sophie."

Their gazes collided and held, the memory of that first day a bond between them.

"I'd never had one before, either."

"We did a great job, though, didn't we? Pretty special watching a life come into the world."

The mare rose slightly on her back legs and heaved. Both humans turned their attention to her as the foal's nose and knees inched forward.

"Amazing. So amazing," she muttered. "Do we need to do anything?"

"Not yet. Let nature take its course." He hitched his chin toward a box residing along the edge of the stall. "Unless she goes too long or has trouble, all we have to do is take care of the foal when he arrives. The kit is ready and waiting if we need it."

Jenna had no idea what was in the kit but was not surprised that Dax was ready for any eventuality. Any man who could help birth a baby by the side of the road could handle anything.

The mare rose slightly and strained.

Jenna gasped. "There's his head. Oh, Dax. Look, there he comes."

Dax, who'd been watching the birth, turned to watch Jenna. Instead of feeling self-conscious, Jenna laughed, happy, excited and filled with wonder as the tiny foal slipped onto the clean straw.

"Oh, oh, oh." Tears filled her eyes. In a voice of wonder, she whispered, "Is he okay?"

It occurred to her then that Dax may have felt this way the day Sophie was born. Anxious and awed and overwhelmed by the beauty of new life.

Dax's voice was soft, too. "Watch his mama work. She knows what to do."

Sure enough, the mare pushed to a stand and turned to her newborn, instinctively stimulating and warming him with her tongue. As she did so, Dax examined the foal, applied antiseptic to the umbilical cord and stepped away, motioning Jenna to join him.

Together they watched the mother care for her baby. When the foal struggled to stand, Jenna's whole body tensed with the effort. "Come on, baby. You can do it."

The spotted foal wobbled up. Jenna turned to Dax, realizing for the first time that she held his hand in a death grip. He smiled into her eyes. She smiled back. He took a step closer. She stood her ground. When his calloused rancher's hand slid beneath her hair and caressed her neck, she shivered. He looked pleased by her reaction. Slowly, he titled her face up and brought his down. Jenna's fingers roamed up the front of his open jacket, over the muscular chest and shoulders to twine in the hair at his nape. She breathed in and let her eyes fall closed as Dax's warm, supple mouth caressed hers.

Sensation washed through her. Desire and hope and love and the belief that this was right and good. He kissed her until her heart hammered in her throat and her knees quivered. When at last the glorious torture ended, he went on holding her in his arms. His breath came in soft rasps against her hair. He took one of her hands and pressed it to his heart. The powerful beat hammered against her palm.

Holding his beautiful green eyes with her gaze, she returned the favor, pressing his big hand to her chest. His nostrils flared and he smiled softly.

Without words, they communicated the flood of emotions rushing in and around them. The feelings were too new and raw to express aloud. At least for Jenna. She wanted to believe she wasn't being a fool and that Dax felt the same.

Behind her, the mare and foal rustled and moved about as the newborn searched for his first meal.

Jenna longed to stay in Dax's warm embrace but a sound from the baby monitor in her pocket ended the moment.

"I should go," she murmured, hearing the tremor in the words.

As he stepped away, Dax dragged a hand over his face and nodded. "Yes. You should. Go."

Jenna tilted her head, trying to gauge his meaning. Gone was the loving look of moments before. An anxious moth fluttered in her chest. What was he not saying?

Maybe he kissed women in the barn all the time. Maybe this meant nothing to him. Maybe she was still the gullible girl that had fallen for Derek.

"Dax?"

He heaved a great sigh. "I apologize. That shouldn't have happened."

He'd kissed her twice in the space of a few hours and it shouldn't have happened? She couldn't believe this.

What was going on inside that complicated head of his?

She stared, waiting with a fragile hope that he would explain.

He clenched his fist and averted his eyes.

Jutting her chin, she said, "No need to apologize. I'm a grown woman and, in case you didn't notice, I was not resisting."

Then with head held high, she rushed outside, the chill in her heart far colder than the December night.

Dax called himself ten kinds of fool and uttered every curse word stored in his memory banks. It was a good thing horses didn't speak English or the mare would have chased him out of the stall.

What had he been thinking to kiss Jenna, not once but twice? The first time he'd convinced himself was to comfort her after the ugly scene with Rowdy. He had no excuse for this second time. He should never have asked her into the barn. He should have left well enough alone. She was his housekeeper, not a girlfriend. His indecently *young* housekeeper.

At least Rowdy was close to her age. Dax had no excuse at all. No excuse except for the fact that he was falling for her. One minute they'd been admiring the new foal, then he'd gazed into those warm brown eyes so filled with the same wonder he always felt at a birthing, and he'd seen a woman after his own heart. A woman who'd returned his kiss with a hungry innocence that turned his insides to jelly. His brain had shorted out. That's all there was to it. He had better self-discipline than to do such a thing.

Anyway, he used to.

No fool like an old fool, Coleman.

He kicked the side of the stall. Pain shot up his leg and he accepted it with a perverse pleasure. The mare turned her head to give him a censorious stare.

"Sorry, old girl." Sorrier than he could ever say.

He cleaned up the stall and after one last examination of mother and baby, he returned to the house.

The tree lights were the only light shining inside the house, and he stood in the entry for several seconds, thinking and admiring the beautiful display. He had erected the tree each year for Gavin's sake but the efforts had been half-hearted. A few ornaments. A few gifts. Gavin's stocking. Jenna had transformed the house into a Christmas wonderland and claimed she wasn't finished yet.

Shucking his boots, he headed for bed, stopping to peek in at Gavin. The night-light—a necessity for his anxious son—illuminated the room enough that he could see the twin bed. The covers were tossed and rumpled but Gavin wasn't there.

His heart leaped. "Gavin?"

He entered the room, flipping on the overhead

light as he moved toward the pile of camouflage-patterned covers. Sure enough Gavin was gone.

Sometimes his son had nightmares and climbed into bed with old dad. Dax stepped to his own room and flipped on the light. Gavin wasn't there, either.

There was only one other place he could be.

With a quick stride, Dax crossed the long ranch house to Jenna's room. He dreaded opening the door and seeing her in the bed, but he needed to know that his son was all right. Just the thought of Jenna in a nightgown with nothing underneath drove his imagination wild. He had enough problems with seeing her in the full-length robe, her pretty toes peeking from beneath.

Like an embattled prizefighter, he shook off the fantasy. Jenna was off-limits. If he was any kind of man, she had to be.

As quietly as possible, he turned the knob and entered the nursery first. Sophie lay on her back, little arms flung up and out. His heart squeezed. Once upon a time he'd dreamed of having a baby girl to call him Daddy. And Sophie had no father to love and protect her.

He watched a moment longer, confident that the pink princess was breathing, and then moved to the connecting doorway. At the sight before him, he squeezed his eyelids tight and let the wave of sweetness take him, if only for a moment.

Forever, he would cherish the mental image of his little boy snuggled safely in Jenna's bed. Her body was spooned around his and her arms held him close, one hand on his chest and the other against his cheek as though reassuring him that she was there and all was well.

The noise on the monitor that had sent her scurrying away from the barn hadn't been her child, as he'd thought. It had been his. And yet Jenna had responded to Gavin's call as though she was his mother.

Dax dragged a weary hand over his face and heard the scratchy beard. Jenna disarmed him. Took away his resistance. Touched him to the very soul.

Ah, God, he loved her. He *loved* her.

He loved her enough to do what was right.

The problem was, he hadn't figured out exactly what that was.

CHAPTER FOURTEEN

"BLAST THIS RAIN. Blast this wasted day." Dax stomped into the mudroom and bent to remove his boots. Water sluiced from his hat and rain slicker onto the tile. He shucked the hat and jacket, too, and took a towel from the overhead cabinet, breathing in the fragrance of fabric softener. That was another of Jenna's touches.

Frustrated, he ground his back teeth. He'd risen before sunrise, having slept little, and hurried out to check the mare and foal. Mostly, he'd hurried out to avoid Jenna and the whirlpool of confused emotions she incited. Now a cold December rain had forced him back inside.

Maybe he should have stayed in the barn all day.

But if he was honest, he missed having breakfast with her, missed seeing Gavin off to school, missed the few minutes of playtime with Sophie.

Jenna rounded the corner, carrying a laundry

basket. Upon spotting him, she stopped dead still. Her eyes widened. One aristocratic eyebrow twitched.

It was a moment he'd both dreaded and longed for.

"Blasted rain," he grumbled, more to avoid the real issues than for conversation.

"You're soaked." She dropped the basket and dug more towels from the cupboard, handing him one and patting his drips with the other. "You're going to be sick."

Her ministrations felt too good, too...wifely.

He took the towel from her. "I got it."

She stood her ground, watching him. "You need to get warm and dry. I have fresh coffee."

"In a minute. I have to change."

"Clean clothes in the dryer," she said and left the room.

Dax stared after her for a few seconds, contemplating the psychology of women. If he lived to a hundred, he would never understand. She didn't seem angry. She didn't seem upset. She didn't seem anything. After his weird behavior last night, she should have tossed him back out in the freezing rain.

He made a self-mocking noise, glanced down

at the pool of water forming around his bare feet and quickly undressed, letting his clothes drop to the floor.

He was standing buck naked in the mudroom while his housekeeper, the woman who was driving him crazy, was in the next room with only a wall between them.

He was chilled to the bone, but his traitorous male body reacted inappropriately anyway. Being a man was an annoyance at times. Jaw clenched, he scavenged in the dryer and sighed with appreciation as he dressed in warm, fragrant clothing.

Once Jenna had gotten the hang of doing laundry, the result was far more pleasant than his pitiful attempts. To his way of thinking, chuck all the clothes in at once and let 'em spin. Jenna's way was magic—and smelled good, too.

Out of long habit, he gathered up the mess in the floor, but the washer was already running, so he dropped them in an empty basket and went in search of that hot coffee.

Jenna wasn't in the kitchen. He wanted to be glad, but instead he poured a steaming mug and went in search of her. Might as well have a little talk, let her know she didn't have to worry about him coming on to her the way Rowdy had. Clear the air.

He found her in the living room, kneeling in front of the fireplace.

"What are you doing?"

She glanced over one shoulder, her hair catching on her mouth. His gaze went straight there as the thought of her kisses came slamming down on him. That puffy bottom lip tasted like sugar and cinnamon and pure delight.

"I thought a fire would be lovely," that mouth said. "And you need to warm up quickly. This is flu season."

His mouth twitched. "Afraid I'll get sick and you'll be stuck taking care of me?"

She studied him solemnly. "Actually, no. I don't want you to miss the Christmas party."

"Ah, yes, the party." He rounded the sectional and set his cup on the table to kneel beside her. Their shoulders brushed and enough electricity arced from his body to start the fire without matches. "Let me help."

She shifted to one side, breaking contact with him, and shoved a handful of crumpled newspaper into the fireplace. "I'm quite capable."

Ah, so she *was* upset with him but too dignified to say so.

Before his brain could engage, he grasped her

hands and turned her toward him. "I apologized last night."

"How rude of you!" Color flared on her cheekbones.

Her abrupt words took him aback. He wasn't sure what response he'd expected but certainly not that one.

"Rude?" Since when was apologizing considered rude?

"A gentleman kisses a woman and then apologizes? What does that say to the woman?"

He blinked, baffled. This was a side of Jenna he hadn't seen.

"It says," she went on in that prissy, citified tone, "that he regrets kissing her. That somehow her kisses were unpleasant."

He blinked like a man staring too long at the sun. "It does?"

She nodded. "Isn't that why you apologized?"

"No. You kiss great. I could have stayed out there all night kissing you. You're amazing."

Her face softened. She pressed her fingertips to her chest. With wonder and hope, she whispered, "I am?"

Dax frowned, swallowing hard. She was confusing him. If he didn't shut up, he'd say something he shouldn't. But he couldn't let her go on thinking she'd done something wrong, either.

"I'm the offender here, Jenna. Not you. You—you're very special." He said the last on a rush of air, wishing the words back but thrilled with the joy that leaped into her expression.

"Oh, Dax." She took his chin in her small, soft fingers and held him captive. "What are you afraid of?"

All his resistance seeped out, as though her touch had the power to disarm every carefully erected defense.

"You," he said simply, quietly. "I'm afraid of you."

Her hand fell away. And oh, he wished it back. He wanted her to go on touching him, making him feel alive and real again in a way he hadn't felt in so long.

Bewildered eyes beseeched him. "I don't understand."

"I know you don't. I know." His throat tightened, full of emotion he shouldn't express. Yet he had to find a way to explain. She'd done nothing but make his life better. She deserved everything good.

Helpless to say anything yet, he pulled her head against his chest. The steady rhythm of his life force beat for her, and he didn't know what to do about it. She felt right in his arms and he wanted her there forever.

Her slender arms snaked around his neck. A wild flurry of hope rose inside him.

He tried to beat it back, tried to deny it existed, and still it fluttered there, as fragile as a new butterfly.

"Talk to me, Dax. Tell me what's going on." Her breath tickled his ear. He heard the hurt and confusion, but he also heard something else—determination and strength.

He realized that this woman-child who'd invaded his life was far stronger than he'd given her credit for. With grit and determination, she'd forged a new life for herself and her baby, taking on the role of his housekeeper when he knew very well that she'd never done this kind of work before. Yet, she'd persevered, and learning fast, had turned the Southpaw Cattle Company into a home filled with love.

He closed his eyes and inhaled her scent. Orange blossoms, she'd told him one day when he'd asked. He loved it. He loved her. She was more woman than his ex had ever been.

"Dax?" she murmured again. Only this time, she

brushed a soft kiss across his cheek as she leaned back on her heels. "Will you please talk to me? Tell me what's going on in that head of yours."

Talk. He wasn't much good at that. How did a man express his feelings and concerns without opening himself up to heartache? How did he do what was best for her and still keep his sanity?

He licked lips gone dry and turned toward the half-laid fire. "Let's get this fire going."

Jenna said nothing but remained there resting on her heels, hands in her lap. She was thinking, though he had no idea where her thoughts were taking her.

Horses and cows he understood, but he'd never quite figured out women.

Intensely aware of her beside him watching, he arranged kindling on the grate, scraped a long fireplace match along the stone hearth and lit the wadded paper. The flame started small but quickly grew to catch the dry pine.

He'd never been much into analogy, but building the fire reminded him of the woman by his side. He'd been as dry as this kindling. Then Jenna had come along, reminded him of his blessings and the joys of everyday living and started a small spark of hope and light inside him. Now that spark had grown into a flame that burned only for her.

He pivoted to reach for a hickory log. Jenna anticipated his needs, as she'd done for weeks now, and handed him the stick of wood.

His hand trembled the slightest bit as he finished laying the fire and sat back to watch the flames climb higher. Heat began to warm his face.

Jenna shifted away and then stood. Dax looked up. "Where are you going?"

Her mouth curved. "I'll be back."

"Promise?" Ah, man, he was a mess.

Her eyes twinkled. "Are you going to talk to me?"

As worried as he was about screwing up everything and causing her to leave, he still found a certain humor in the situation. "Are you going to nag me if I don't?"

This time she laughed. "What do you think?" And then she hurried out of the living room.

Dax set the fire screen in place, dusted his hands down the sides of his clean jeans and looked around the living room. The place was magazine beautiful since Jenna had rearranged furniture and accessories, added pictures and doodads to the walls and gone all out for Christmas. She'd added a pair of enormous floor pillows for Gavin to flop on when he watched TV. Dax took those now and fluffed them onto the rug in front of the fire, refusing to examine the reasons behind the action.

"Here we go, sir," Jenna said. He scowled at her. The term *sir* didn't sit too well, considering the battle raging inside him. He didn't need any reminders that she was his employee and that he was twelve years older.

Furry slippers snip-snapping against her heels, she came toward him carrying a tray which she deposited on the coffee table. The scent of cinnamon wafted up from a plate piled high with ornament cookies. The tray was jammed with paintbrushes, tiny bowls of colored frosting and red ribbon.

"Are you putting me to work?"

"This is on my to-do list today. I thought you might like to decorate some while you bask by the fireside. It's fun."

Bask by the fireside? Her words tickled him. "What about Gavin?"

"I saved a plate for him. He gets tired after five or six."

Well, decorating cookies wasn't the kind of thing he'd had in mind, but he had to admit her idea was better than his. Cozying up with Jenna in front of a fire could be a dangerous proposition.

"Sophie asleep?" he asked, taking up a paint brush.

"Midmorning nap. Crystal said some babies don't adjust to a schedule right away, but Sophie has. She's the most amazing baby." The light of mother-love warmed her face. Dax's insides squeezed with gladness for Sophie. His baby had never had that kind of female devotion.

A voice in his head said, "Until now," and the vision of Jenna curved protectively, lovingly around his boy rose in his mind.

Taking up a Santa-shaped ornament, he dipped his brush in red frosting. "You gonna tell me about Gavin's nightmare?"

Brush and cookie in hand, she looked at him in surprise. "How did you know?"

"When I came in from the barn, I checked on him." He shrugged. "Always do. He was gone. You heard him on the monitor, didn't you? That's why you came inside last night."

Jenna tilted her head.

Yes, she'd come in for that reason, but also because he'd kissed her and then pushed her away. She was still pondering that turn of events.

"I'm not sure what he dreamed," she said. "But he was shivering and scared."

"Thank you for looking after him."

"No gratitude is required, Dax." Jenna dropped her gaze to the gingerbread boy. "I love him."

There, she'd admitted her love for one of the Coleman men. One down and one to go.

Dax didn't respond to the declaration, just went on painting Santa's hat with red frosting.

After a bit, he said, "You know I'm divorced."

The topic surprised her a little, but she was ready to hear the story from him. "Yes."

"Gavin never really knew his mother. She left when he was a few days old." He laid aside the paintbrush and drew in a deep breath. "She never wanted him."

"How horrible. He doesn't know, does he?"

"No. No. I'd never tell him such a thing, but he has to feel it. Other boys have mothers and he has never even seen his. When he was three years old, he began to notice that baby horses have mamas. Baby calves have mamas. Even his dad has a mama. Now that he's started school, he talks about it more. He's more clingy and the nightmares come more often." He rubbed the side of his neck as though the worry gave him a pain. "I don't know what to do."

"His lack of a mother is not your fault."

"I feel as if it is. I wasn't the best husband in the world. Always working, constantly out in the barn or the fields or off to stock sales and shows."

He looked so sad Jenna couldn't stop herself. She put aside her decorations, reached across the table and touched the back of his hand. "You were making a living for your family. That's as it should be."

"Reba didn't think so. She wanted parties and travel and fun."

"Nothing wrong with those things."

"That's why I blame myself."

"You didn't understand my meaning. There is nothing wrong with those things in small increments, but they aren't a lifestyle. Or they shouldn't be." No one knew that better than her. "My husband was the same way. Life was a party." As long as she was paying the bills and didn't stand in the way.

"Did you love him?"

She lifted a shoulder. "I thought I did. Did you love Reba?"

He nodded. "Yeah. Too much, I guess."

The admission poked at Jenna like a pinprick.

"I need you to know something," he went on.

"She started divorce proceedings long before Gavin was born." His Adam's apple rose and fell. "After I caught her in bed with my brother."

The stark pain on his face drove the breath from her lungs. She knew that kind of betrayal, too, although she'd never caught Derek in the act. The newspaper speculation had been humiliating enough.

"You must have been…shattered."

"Yeah. We had just found out she was pregnant. I was overjoyed—and too stupid to see what was going on under my nose. I thought she was finally ready to settle down."

"I'm sorry."

"You know the last words she said to me?" His jaw worked, his fist tightened beneath her fingers, and Jenna could feel the rage and hurt coming off him in waves. "She asked me if I'd always wonder for certain if the kid she'd given me was really mine."

Jenna had never been a violent person, but she wanted to slap a certain female named Reba. The woman was too cruel for words. "Do you?"

He shook his head. "No. Oh, I thought about it when she first left, but after a while I no longer cared. I believe he's mine by biology, but even if he isn't, he's mine in here." He tapped a finger to his breastbone. "I rocked him, walked the floor with him, diapered his bottom and spooned baby food into his bird mouth. With every new thing I did for and with my son, I loved him deeper. He's a trooper, a hearty little soul who survived a stumbling, bumbling daddy. I just wish I could have been a mama to him, too. How could she do that to him? How could she not love a son like Gavin?"

"I don't understand, either, Dax."

He turned his hand over and clasped her palm in his. "I know you don't. That's one of the things I—admire about you."

Jenna heard the hesitation in his speech. Had he almost said love? Her pulse quivered in her chest, a hopeful bird fluttering for release.

Dax had been badly wounded and now she understood that those wounds made him cautious. She wanted to reassure him that she would never hurt him that way. She wanted him to know that the longing to mother Gavin grew stronger every day.

But she didn't tell him. She couldn't. Yet.

Dax took up the paintbrush and cookie again. "This is supposed to be a fun rainy-day project. Didn't mean to get serious on you."

"I asked you to talk to me." The man needed a

partner to share his heavy load. And she needed to be needed. For most of her life, she'd been nothing but an ornament like the ones on the massive Christmas tree. Having Sophie and being a part of Dax's life had given her a sense of worth.

He turned the cinnamon cookie in her direction. "What do ya think of Santa?"

So he didn't want to discuss his ex-wife anymore. She understood. Derek wasn't her favorite topic, either. But she did want Dax to have some fun for a change.

She wrinkled her nose. "I thought Santa's boots were black."

Dax made a silly face. "Oops. I'll fix it."

When he leaned in to dip the brush in black frosting, Jenna dabbed paint on the tip of his nose.

"Oh, my goodness," she said with mock seriousness. "You have frosting on your nose."

"I do?" he asked in the same silly tone she'd used. All the while he swirled his paintbrush round and round in the frosting bowl. "Ever heard of face painting?"

Jenna dotted a gingerbread boy with white icing eyes. "Don't they do that at fairs and carnivals?"

Such events were below the status of a Carrington, but she'd seen the activity on television and had envied those lucky children their flowers and cartoon characters.

"And in living rooms on rainy days," he said.

Her gaze flew up to meet his. "Truly?"

He laughed and pointed the brush at her. "First time for everything. What do ya say, Jenna, want to launch my art career?"

She held up a warning finger. "Don't even think about it."

"Too late." Mischief filled his face.

"Dax," she warned, though the rise of energy inside her and the giggle she couldn't stop gave the lie to her warning.

"Ah, come on, Jenna. Play nice. Let me decorate your face. A few dots here, a blue stripe there. Gonna be fantastic." On his knees, he walked toward her, frosting near the drip stage.

"Don't you dare." She crab-crawled backward, but Dax kept coming, brush loaded with bright blue paint.

Like the villain in an old-time movie, he pumped his eyebrows. If he'd had a mustache, he would probably have twirled the ends, too.

Giggling, Jenna scooted back some more, though she couldn't escape—even if she'd wanted to.

Dax pounced. Jenna flung an arm upward to

ward off the blue-drenched brush. Bits of cookie paint flicked loose. A laughing, halfhearted wrestling match ensued, but Jenna was no match for the big man's superior strength. In two seconds flat she was pinned to the floor, her wrists manacled above her head by one of his powerful hands while the other advanced toward her face with a glob of shiny blue frosting. Jenna switched her head from side to side, laughing so hard now that she could barely breathe.

When Dax saw that he couldn't paint a face in motion, he resorted to threats. "Take your punishment or prepare to wash sugar out of your hair."

She stilled but couldn't stop giggling as Dax moved closer with the brush. She'd never seen him playful. He was still a young man but the past and his load of responsibility weighed him down. He needed to laugh and feel young and happy again. And she was thrilled to be a part of the moment— even if it meant having her cheek painted.

But instead of dabbing her cheek, Dax stroked the brush over her mouth. The motion tickled, but Jenna stopped giggling. A tingle of awareness moved from her mouth into her chest and lower.

She became acutely cognizant of Dax's body pressing into hers in all the right places.

"You have the most gorgeous mouth," he murmured.

She tried to joke. "And you think it should be painted blue?"

A tiny smile played at the corners of his mouth as he slowly outlined her top lip with the fine-tipped brush. She shivered. He raised his eyes to hers and then went back to his beguiling work. With painstaking care, while she throbbed at his nearness, he outlined her bottom lip, then dipped his brush again and filled in every millimeter of her mouth.

By now her heart thundered in her ears. Though she tried to control her breathing, her chest rose and fell more quickly. Her tongue snaked out to moisten lips gone dry from nerves and drying sugar. As if she'd issued a command, Dax tossed the brush aside and leaned in to nibble at the corner of her mouth.

"Yum," he said, his breath stirring the sensitive tissues, making her yearn.

She tried to move, to turn her lips into his, but he backed away a fraction of an inch. His eyelids were hooded and sexy.

"Be still." The gravelly command raised goose bumps on her arms. Dax noticed and laughed softly. "I made this mess. I'll clean it up."

While Jenna thought she'd die if he didn't kiss her right then, she played his sensual game. His hot, enticing tongue followed the path of the paintbrush around her lips.

"Sweet as sugar," he murmured, the words flowing into her mouth from his. She smiled a little at the joke.

He nibbled her bottom lip. She let her mouth drop open slightly hoping he'd take the hint.

But Dax was not finished with his delicious torture. He went right on nipping and tasting, making soft moaning sounds that sent her blood racing and alerted every nerve ending in her body.

The taste of sugar mingled with the coffee they'd drunk and a taste that only belonged to Dax—manly, hot and yet cautious as though he was holding himself in check. She didn't want caution. She wanted him.

"Dax," she whispered in a shaky voice.

He raised his head and their eyes locked. The desire she saw there didn't surprise her, but the tenderness did. For all his gruffness, Dax had a way of making her feel cherished.

"I—I—" She longed to admit her love but there were other things she had to tell him first. And yet if she discussed her past, this beautiful spell would be broken. She couldn't bear if he was angry with her for keeping the secret. Not today when she felt more beautiful and special than she'd ever felt in her life. So in the end, she closed her eyes and said nothing. Dax didn't move and she could feel his gaze boring into her. His breath soughed gently and after a moment he shifted slightly, though he never released her hands. He held her captive with his fingers, his body and his lips. She wondered if he knew that he also held her captive with his heart.

Her lips dropped open and this time Dax took full advantage to devour the remaining sugar, caressing her mouth until she thought she might melt into the carpet.

He worked his way over her chin and jaw and to her ear where he puffed softly until she shivered, and then he kissed his way down her throat. It was then he loosened his hold on her wrists. With deep pleasure humming through her body, she laced her fingers in his thick hair and drew him closer.

Just when Jenna thought she would combust with desire, Sophie let out a howl.

Both adults froze. The only sounds in the room were the crackle of the fireplace and the pounding of their hearts.

Sophie cried out again.

Dax growled deep in his throat, and then he chuckled. The sound vibrated inside Jenna's chest. With a wry grin, he rolled to one side and helped her sit up. "Saved by the baby."

She hadn't wanted to be saved from Dax, but common sense would say to take things slowly. She pushed to a stand, using Dax's broad shoulder for leverage. Her knees trembled. "It's time for her bottle."

"Bring her in here." He shoved a hand through his hair, forking it up in all directions. "I missed playtime this morning."

Jenna studied him. He wasn't angry. A little frustrated perhaps, but not angry. Instead he wanted to spend time with her and Sophie.

How could she not love a man like that?

CHAPTER FIFTEEN

Dax lifted the lid on the stew pot and sniffed. Steam and the aroma of chicken broth warmed his face. Jenna had gone into town for lunch with Crystal and a couple of other girlfriends, leaving the stew pot for his lunch. According to Jenna, they were revising a guest list for the Christmas party that seemed to grow larger each day. Not that he minded. If having a party made her happy, she could have one every day.

Taking a thick stoneware bowl from the shelf, he dipped it full of the Brunswick Stew, sliced a chunk of corn bread and settled in at the bar for lunch.

The rainy day had changed everything. He could no more explain it than he could explain why a woman like Jenna Garwood would choose to remain on the Southpaw with him and Gavin, but he felt more positive about life than he had in years. Hope was a magical emotion and he was filled with it.

As much as he'd wanted to make love to Jenna that day, he now knew the timing had been wrong. They were still learning and growing together and each day was a discovery. Jenna in his kitchen. Jenna in his living room. Jenna dancing in circles to Christmas music with Sophie in her arms.

He loved sneaking up behind her when she was busy. He'd plant a kiss on her neck or her hair and she'd spin around, face flushed, to fall against him for a real kiss.

Sometimes at night when he crawled into the king-size bed, he let himself imagine what it would be like if Jenna was lying beside him. They'd talk about the day's events, laugh at things the kids had done, and then make love sweeter than any cookie frosting ever created.

He spooned the thick soup into his mouth and moaned with appreciation. His Jenna was a fine chef. *His* Jenna. Was she? Did she want to be? He thought she did but he had to be sure. *She* had to be sure.

She was in his house and in his heart. He wanted her in his bed, too.

Making love didn't scare him. Falling in love did.

They'd never spoken of age, but that rainy day in her arms had convinced him that Jenna was far more woman than girl. Part of him still worried that he was too old, too broken and too bitter to give a young, vibrant woman what she needed.

But hope had come to the Southpaw and Dax clung to it like a drowning man to a bit of flotsam. For indeed, he'd been dead inside when Jenna Garwood and her baby had opened the door to his empty heart and made themselves welcome.

Though still convinced that she had secrets, he was afraid to ask. What if he didn't like the answers? What if he drove her away? For now, he couldn't take the chance. Maybe by spring, he'd be more confident—if he could keep his libido in check that long. Jenna deserved more than an employer who took advantage.

He slathered butter on his corn bread and bit down. Jenna had never before baked corn bread but when he'd mentioned a fondness for the Southern dish, it had appeared at the next meal, just the way he liked it with a touch of sugar. He took another bite and realized he was smiling.

She'd left the Christmas tree lights on and last night, she and Gavin had hung the elaborately quilted and personalized stockings on the gleaming wood mantel. The house was alive with her special touches.

Outside he heard the sound of a car and his heart leaped. Jenna must be back early. Forgetting all about his half-eaten meal, he shoved off the bar stool and hurried to the door. Though she'd only been gone a couple of hours, he missed her.

He yanked the front door open and paused. A long, sleek, black car pulled into his drive. No one he knew drove a car of that caliber, at least not out here in the country. This looked like something a government official would drive.

A sense of foreboding crawled up the back of his neck. He shook it off.

A uniformed driver complete with a flat cap like something out of a movie, exited the car and opened the back door. With a stiff bow, the chauffeur extended a hand to assist the occupant. Out stepped a dark-haired, middle-aged woman in a crisp tan suit. Nose high, she gazed around, taking in the brown landscape and finally coming to rest on him. She looked him over and then squared her shoulders and said something to the chauffeur. From the other side of the car, a burly man exited and came around to stand beside the elegantly clad woman. To Dax's way of thinking, the man looked like a cop—or a gangster.

Normally, Dax went out to greet his company, but something about this group bothered him. He didn't know them, but something didn't feel right.

The dark-haired woman and the burly man came toward the house. Dax stepped out onto the porch.

"You folks lost?"

"I think not." The woman's voice was high-brow and disdaining. "This is the Southpaw Cattle Company, isn't it?"

"It is."

"And may I inquire as to who you are?"

Both the phrasing and the accent sounded eerily familiar. "Dax Coleman. This is my place. And you are?"

"Elaine Carrington. May I come inside please? We have some business to discuss."

He couldn't imagine what business he could possibly have with a woman he'd never heard of but he motioned toward the house. "Come on in."

He led the way, taking note that the burly fellow followed but hadn't been introduced. The man cast a suspicious eye in all directions as they entered the foyer and passed into the living room.

"Have a seat," Dax said. He waited as politely as

possible while the woman settled on the divan and then he perched on the edge of a nearby chair. The burly man didn't sit, rather took up residence at the end of the couch, his arms crossed over his chest.

What was this guy anyway? Some kind of bodyguard?

"I'll get straight to the point," the woman said. "I'm looking for my daughter, Genevieve Carrington."

Dax relaxed the slightest bit. For a minute there, he was scared she was going to mention Jenna. "Sorry, ma'am. I don't know her."

The woman's lips thinned. "That's not what my sources tell me."

Dax was stricken with an overpowering need to get these strangers off his land. "Well, your sources are wrong. So if you'll excuse me, I have a ranch to run."

"Just a moment, Mr. Coleman. I've spent thousands of dollars tracking my daughter. I know she's been here. I know she gave birth to a daughter—my grandchild—in the local hospital. I also know she took a position with your ranch—" her nostrils flared in distaste "—as a domestic."

Oh no. No.

Dax wanted to put a hand over her mouth and

stop the flow of words but instead he sat frozen like a plastic snowman.

Mrs. Carrington opened her black leather bag and withdrew a paper which she handed to Dax. "This photo was taken shortly before her husband died."

Before he even looked down, Dax knew who would be smiling out at him, but his heart dropped anyway.

"Jenna," he said. "My housekeeper's name is Jenna Garwood, not Carrington."

"So she is here. Thank God." A world of tension left the woman's body. "Garwood was her married name. Where is she? Where is my grand-daughter? We need to get them back to Pennsylvania under medical care right away."

Dax's pulse jumped. "Is Jenna sick?"

"Of course she is. What person in her right mind would run away from her family estate in the ninth month of pregnancy and leave behind a multimillion dollar trust fund?"

His ears buzzed. He could have sworn she said Jenna was rich. "If that's true, why did she come to work here?"

"My point exactly. Jenna is the sole heiress to a vast fortune. Since her husband's death, she has not been well. I blame myself for not getting her the help she needed sooner. Haven't you ever heard of postpartum depression? Hormonal psychosis? Our physician believes this is likely the culprit, and now that she has delivered the baby, the danger increases. So please, Mr. Coleman, tell me where my daughter is so we can take her home where she belongs."

Dax ran a shaky hand over his face. He couldn't believe this. He was living in a nightmare. Jenna, his love, the woman he wanted to keep forever, obviously didn't feel the same. She'd had plenty of chances to tell him who she was, and she hadn't.

He felt as if his heart would burst right out of his chest. What an idiot he was to think a woman like Jenna could care for him. He'd known from the beginning she didn't fit in his world. She was too young, too classy. The warning signs were all around him, and yet he'd shut them out.

The rumble of a car engine sounded, growing closer. His gut knotted to the point of nausea. He had to get out of here before he did something he'd regret forever. Call him a coward, but he couldn't look into Jenna's eyes without losing his cool. It wasn't so much that she hadn't told him, it was that she hadn't trusted him. And more than that, her mother was right. Jenna was a blue blood. She shouldn't be scrubbing floors for a Texas rancher.

"That's Jenna's car," he said, somehow managing to force the words past the knot in his throat. "If you'll excuse me, I'll leave you to your reunion."

With a curt nod, he took his hat and coat and exited out the back way.

They had found her.

The moment she turned down the graveled drive into the Southpaw, Jenna went weak all over. Though she didn't recognize the black luxury sedan parked next to the house, she recognized the Carrington style.

She tapped the brake, blood roaring in her head as she contemplated the best mode of action. If the visitor was, indeed, Mother, she'd already spoken to Dax. By now, he'd be wondering what kind of crazy person would run away from a fortune. Worse yet, he'd be wondering why Jenna had kept such a secret from him even after their relationship had begun to flower.

Now she wondered the same thing. She should have told him. She should have explained about the years of living an overprotected life with a neurotic mother whose fears controlled her every movement.

The memory of her miserable childhood stiffened her spine. She was an adult. Her mother could not force her to return home.

She pulled into the garage, gathered Sophie into her arms and let herself in through the back door. She could hear the clip of her mother's voice speaking to someone.

Holding her baby close, knees trembling, she moved quietly down the hall and through the house until she stood in the entry between the dining and living rooms.

"Hello, Mother." Jenna's voice sounded cool, but her insides wobbled.

"Jenna, darling." Elaine rose and reached toward her. Jenna remained aloof and on guard, but an unexpected surge of emotion struck her. Tears pressed at the back of her eyelids. As damaged as their relationship was, she'd missed her family.

Elaine moved forward to touch the white blanket surrounding Sophie. "Is this our little Rose Elizabeth?"

The moment of weakness fled. Her mother had insisted Jenna name her baby after two matriarchs of the Carrington family, considering her choice far more fitting than anything Jenna suggested. Elaine had even preenrolled Sophie in an elite private school under that name and against Jenna's wishes.

"Her name is Sophie Joy."

Elaine drew back, startled that her will had been questioned, but as "befitting one of her station," she quickly masked her real feelings.

"Sit down, darling. You look terrible." She glanced at Parm, head of Carrington security for as long as Jenna could remember. "Don't you agree, Parm? She's clearly been ill."

Parm inclined his head, agreeing as always with his employer.

"I've never been healthier, Mother."

"Don't try to hide the truth from me, darling. I know when something's wrong." She tilted Jenna's face upward and studied her as if she were a painting. "If you would only have told your father or me how distraught you were over Derek's death and—well, that other distasteful affair, we would have gotten you the help you needed."

Leave it to mother to consider death and adultery as equally distasteful. "The situation with Derek was only one of the reasons I left. I don't expect you to understand. But I do expect you to get in your car, return to the airport and go home."

"Not without you and my granddaughter." Elaine smoothed the back of her skirt and reseated herself. "You're ill. You have been for some time."

"You want me to be ill so you can control me. And Sophie."

"Don't be ridiculous. Genevieve, darling, do you have any heart at all? Don't you realize the terror and despair your father and I experienced when we realized you were gone? We thought our worst nightmare had finally come to pass." She paused, pressed a pampered hand to her heart and closed her eyes. "I wept for days, waiting for the ransom call, certain some vicious monster had stolen my only child."

Jenna's conscience pricked. The Carringtons feared kidnapping above all things. "I left a note."

"A note could have easily been forced from you at gunpoint. Even Parm was deeply concerned that something untoward had occurred."

Jenna swallowed. "I'm sorry, Mother. I never meant to worry you."

"Don't you see, darling, your behavior has been unbalanced, a danger to you and my grandchild."

"I'm a good mother."

"Your love is not in question, but your emotional health is. Now that I'm here I see for myself how desperate the situation is. You look dreadful, exhausted, weathered like a common street urchin. And those hands, your once-beautiful hands…" Her mother's voice trailed away as she stared at Jenna's chipped fingernails.

"I work for a living."

Elaine placed the back of her hand against her forehead as if a migraine was coming on. "Clearly another symptom of how ill you are. Our kind do not work for a living. We serve others in charitable duties. Jenna, child, as difficult as it may be for you to think rationally, consider the things you've done. You engaged in an ill-begotten alliance with a gold-digging philanderer and got yourself pregnant. That alone shows very poor judgment. Then only days before that baby's birth, you disappeared, putting both your child and yourself in jeopardy. Anything could have happened. Dear heavens above, you gave birth to the Carrington heir on the side of the road. You could have died. Don't you understand how terribly ill you must be to have done such a dangerous thing?"

Jenna's heart sank lower than the Texas sun. She had never looked at the situation quite this way. Was Mother right? Had running away been the sign of a mental illness?

"I'm sorry, Mother," she said again and heard the voice of a little girl who had always apologized and obeyed. Five minutes in the company of her mother and Jenna was a child again. Growing more confused and uncertain by the minute, she felt herself weakening.

Perhaps she should go home. Perhaps she wasn't well. Sophie deserved to grow up in a healthy environment. She reached down to smooth the soft cap of blond curls and stared into her baby's eyes. What was the right thing to do for Sophie?

Elaine touched her shoulder, though Jenna hadn't seen her leave the chair. "Come on, darling. Let's get your things and leave before that cowboy person returns."

Like a remote control doll, Jenna rose, clutching Sophie to her breast. "I have to say goodbye."

Elaine took her elbow. "I don't think that's a good idea. Mr. Coleman was very upset."

She blinked. "He was?"

"There's no predicting what he might do now that he knows you're an heiress. Extortion, blackmail. Anything is possible."

Something clicked inside Jenna's brain. "Dax isn't like that. Dax is—" A flood of emotion rushed through her at the thought of everything she'd shared with the Texas rancher.

Here on the Southpaw with Dax, she'd changed from a frightened runaway to an adult with the strength and good sense to run a household, nurture her child as well as his, and turn a lonely house into a lively, beautiful home filled with love. Thanks to Dax, she'd learned that her value and worth had nothing to do with a trust fund. Here she loved and was loved for who she was inside.

Suddenly she knew her mother was wrong. Neither depressed nor mentally ill, Jenna Garwood had become a woman in control of her own life. And she wanted that life to be here, on the Southpaw with Dax if he'd have her. "I love him."

Elaine's head snapped back. "Don't be a fool again. You know what happened the last time a man discovered your trust fund."

Jenna shook her head slowly from side to side as hope returned, a gentle salve to her wounded soul. "He didn't know. He didn't know and he loves me anyway."

He'd never said as much but she knew now.

Dax loved her and Sophie. His love was there in everything he said and did.

She wouldn't go back. She would not allow the Carrington money to ruin Sophie's childhood the way it had ruined hers. She'd run away for Sophie's sake, not to cause her harm, and no amount of psychological manipulation by her mother would change her mind.

Right then, she knew what she had to do.

"Mother, I love and respect you, but I am a grown woman. I am not returning to Pennsylvania." Regardless of what happened with Dax, she could not go home again. "If you wish to be a part of my life and Sophie's, you'll do so under my rules."

Elaine's mouth dropped open. Parm snapped to attention but Jenna knew he wouldn't stop her. He couldn't.

"Now if you will excuse me, Sophie and I have some unfinished business to attend to." With a song in her heart and head held high, she went in search of Dax. Somehow she would make him understand.

CHAPTER SIXTEEN

Dax saw her round the corner of the barn and come toward him across the dead grass, purpose in her stride. The hood of her coat had fallen and her hair blew away from her face. The cold air tinged her cheeks with rose, giving her an invigorated, healthy look. She was carrying the baby bundled in a thick blanket. As she drew near, he could see the excitement emanating from her like heat from a summer sidewalk.

He knew. She was coming to tell him goodbye. She was heading back to the fancy life where she belonged.

Dax hurt so bad he didn't have the strength to cuss. He was breaking in half, shattered at the thought of losing this woman that he'd known all along he shouldn't fall for. And yet he had.

When Reba left, he'd been furious and bitter. But with Jenna, he was simply broken. She'd done nothing but make his life better. She'd driven out the bitterness and replaced it with soft smiles, lobster croquettes and Christmas decorations. And the best kisses a man could fantasize about.

Ah, man, he loved her. Maybe if he'd told her and held her and promised her the moon…ah, what was he thinking? She could buy the moon for herself. She didn't need him.

"Dax?" she said, coming to a halt at his side. He should be angry, but he couldn't muster the energy. He looked down into those brown eyes and fell apart. Dropping the wrench he'd been using to hang the metal gate, he pulled her and Sophie gently into his embrace.

"I'll never forget you, Jenna," he said, memorizing the scent and silkiness of her hair and the curve of her body. Long after she was gone from his life, he wanted to remember. "Gavin will miss you. I hope you'll keep in touch. For his sake."

She stilled. "What about you? Will you miss me?"

He squeezed his eyes against the question. Jenna wasn't normally a cruel person.

"Yeah," he answered raggedly. "I'll miss you, too."

Jenna's body began to tremble. Dax held her tighter. Soft weeping filled his ears. Gripping her upper arms, he put her a little away from him. Tears flowed down her face and dripped onto Sophie's blanket.

"What? Why are you crying?"

"Because I think you love me."

So that was it. She knew he'd fallen hard, and tenderhearted Jenna felt bad about hurting him. But Dax refused to lie about something as precious as love.

He tilted her chin. "You stole my heart the day we brought Sophie into this world. And every day since then I've fallen more in love than I ever dreamed possible."

More tears gushed from her eyes, down her cheeks and into the corners of her mouth. It was all he could do not to kiss them away.

"What would a beautiful angel like you want with me? But I don't regret one moment we spent together. And if I could have one wish in this world—" He stopped, too emotional to go on.

Still weeping softly, Jenna turned her face into his palm and kissed him. The sweetness of that act nearly brought him to his knees.

"Tell me your wish."

He shook his head. "No. I won't put any more

guilt on you. Go home with your family and be happy, Jenna. That's what I wish for you."

The baby had grown restless while the adults talked and let out a whimper. Thinking this was the last time he'd get to hold her, Dax took Sophie and rested her against his shoulder. She settled instantly and if possible Dax's heart broke a little more. He'd fallen for this baby girl as surely as he'd fallen for the mother.

Jenna smiled through her tears and gripped the lapel of his work coat.

"I *am* home with my family, Dax."

He wasn't sure he understood. "Aren't you going back East with your mother?"

Her face crumpled again. "Do you want me to?"

"No!" he shouted.

Sophie jumped and started to cry. Dax patted her back and made a shushing sound until she settled again.

"I mean," he said more quietly, "I want you to do what's best for you. I won't stand in your way." Even if it killed him. "But tell me one thing, why weren't honest with me from the start?"

"I'm sorry. I wish I had been." So did he. "But I was so very afraid."

"Of me?"

"Yes, and of my own inadequacies. Mostly I feared being found by my family and having Sophie taken away."

"I don't understand."

"I know you don't. Unless you've lived in a gilded cage, you can't imagine what it's like. All my life, I've been nothing but a trust fund baby, controlled, overprotected, and only accepted for my fortune. The one time I tried to break away, I chose a man who claimed to love me until he had his hands on my money. And then I was nothing. Nothing."

"You thought I'd care about your blasted fortune!" The idea infuriated him.

"Derek did."

"I'm not him."

"Exactly. You didn't know and you loved me anyway. You saw me and accepted me for who I am in here." She tapped her chest. "Do you know what that means to me? For the first time in my life, I'm a normal person, living a free, happy life. That's what I want. That's what Sophie deserves. Don't you see? I could never subject my daughter to that smothering lifestyle where she never really knows someone else's motives. I want her to have confidence that she can do things for herself, that she can earn her own way, that she's beautiful and special for herself, not her money. I want her to grow up where she was born, surrounded by the simple life and good people of Saddleback."

Wonder and hope began to warm his frozen blood. "You want to go on as my housekeeper? You? A woman who could buy this place and hire a dozen servants?"

Her eyes flashed fire. If he'd been kindling, she would have incinerated him.

Hands on hips, she said, "For a smart man, you can sure act dumb. If that's all you want from me, tell me now and I will leave. Because I don't want to be your housekeeper."

"What do you want?"

She slashed at the tears that had begun again. "I want to love you every day of my life. I want to be your partner and your friend and—"

Before she could finish, he used his free hand to yank her against him. His heart banged against his rib cage like hail on a tin roof. "And my lover and my wife?"

She raised her face to his, eyes red-rimmed but glowing with joy. "Yes!"

With a fierce groan of relief, he kissed the lips he craved. For the rest of his life, he'd remember the feel of the December chill seeping through his clothes, the smell of wood smoke in the air, and the taste of her salty tears…mingling with his.

EPILOGUE

CARS LINED THE YARD and driveway of the Southpaw Cattle Company. Jenna's Christmas Eve party was in full swing and she was so excited and happy she could hardly think straight.

The house was full of friends and Dax's family, who'd driven up from Austin for the holiday. She'd been a little nervous about meeting them, but they seemed to like her and were taken captive by Sophie. Even now, the baby, dressed in a red velvet Mrs. Santa suit, was being passed from person to person.

"The house is gorgeous, hon," Crystal said, coming up from behind with a mini quiche in one hand and a glass of wassail in the other.

"So are you." The darkly pretty nurse had chosen a body-skimming dress in Christmas red, a color that suited her perfectly.

"Joe can't keep his hands off me." Crystal

giggled and waved at her husband, a quiet guy as blond as Crystal was dark.

"Who can blame him?"

"Same with your man. Look at him over there by the canapés, watching your every move. I think he could gobble you up in one bite."

Jenna blushed, tingling with anticipation at what was to come before this night was over. Dax had gone cross-eyed when she'd slid into the barely silver one-shouldered dress and strappy stilettos. "I think I just might let him, too."

Crystal's eyes widened and she laughed. A pair of snowflake earrings danced against her dark skin. "You two are perfect together. I'm thrilled for both of you."

Jenna's heart beat a happy rhythm. "Me, too. The day I crashed my car into Dax's fence, I never dreamed how wonderfully my life would work out."

"You seemed so lost and scared that day, but gritty and determined, too. I knew you were gonna make it. But I have to admit things turned out better than I thought." She sipped her steaming wassail and then whispered, "But the Gucci purse should have given me a clue."

"I'm sorry for keeping that from you."

Jenna had shared the truth about her wealthy

family with Crystal, but she was still determined to live a normal life and put the trust fund money to use for others less blessed.

"Trust me, girl. I totally understand." She hunched her shoulders and grinned. "Well, sort of. The emotional part anyway, but money and Crystal are soon parted. Oops, I see that hunky husband of mine coming my way. Bet he wants to find a dark corner and make out." She popped the remaining quiche into her cherry-colored lips and waved two fingers. "Ta-ta."

Heart glad, Jenna waved and continued her journey through the partygoers, stopping to chat with first one and then another. Gavin's teacher was there, looking cute and young in a Santa hat. Her little girl was twirling in circles to *The Nutcracker* music playing softly through the sound system.

Talk of the weather and Christmas, politics and children, and lots of laughter mingled with the clink of glasses and the smells of pine and cinnamon. It was a good party. People seemed to be enjoying themselves.

But the best was yet to come.

Gradually, she made her way to Dax's side. He was deep in conversation with another rancher about an upcoming stock show in Fort Worth. As soon as he saw her, Dax said to the other man, "'Scuse me, Jake. There's a beautiful woman wanting my attention."

Jake clapped him on the shoulder. "Talk to you later, then. Great party, ma'am."

Jenna smiled her thanks as he moved away.

Dax slid an arm around her waist and nuzzled her ear. "You smell good. Look good, too."

"Ready for our surprise?"

"Can't wait." He stroked the sensitive flesh on the back of her neck. "I'm sorry your parents chose not to come."

With Dax at her side, she'd talked again with her mother and hammered out a fragile truce. Though Elaine would never fully understand, Jenna hoped to build a workable relationship with her family. She loved them. She just couldn't live with them anymore. When they'd been invited to the wedding, however, they'd refused, certain Jenna was making another mistake. She'd been disappointed, though she'd expected the response.

"Someday, they'll realize. But until they do, I refuse to let them ruin tonight."

"I love you." He kissed her cheek.

"I love you, too."

"Come on, then. Let's find our boy." They glanced around the crowded room and located Gavin easily. Reindeer antlers poked up from his dark head. He'd insisted on wearing a brown suit and antlers in honor of Rudolph who, he was convinced, would be stopping at the house later tonight.

"You painted his nose." Dax said, eyes twinkling.

"He asked."

"I wasn't complaining. I was remembering. You. Me. A lot of sugary frosting." He nuzzled her ear again and whispered. "Very soon, I'm going to paint you all over, just so I can clean up the mess."

She gave him a sultry look and twitched one eyebrow. "Ready when you are, cowboy."

His pupils dilated until the green irises were but a rim around the edges. "How about now?"

She laughed, feeling beautiful and sexy and desirable. Dax had done that for her, given her the confidence to be a woman. "How about you get the real party started and we'll save the good stuff for later."

"As my lady wishes." He executed an elegant bow and led her to a roped-off area in front of the crackling fireplace. Guests assumed she'd been protecting the white rug, but she and Dax had other plans. Dax's family already knew and when they spotted Dax and Jenna, they moved into action.

Within minutes, the houselights came down and the glow of the tree, the candles and the fireplace filled the vast room with a festive, romantic glow. A hush came over the guests as they turned in curiosity.

Holding Jenna's hand, Dax stood with his back to the stone fireplace, surrounded by flickering candlelight as he spoke. "Friends and family, Jenna and I have a surprise for you tonight. You've come to celebrate Christmas with us, but we also invited you here for another, more personal reason." He glanced her way and she smiled, certain she radiated enough love and joy to light the darkness all by herself. "Jenna Garwood, this gorgeous, classy, incredible woman has agreed to be my wife."

A murmur of excitement rushed through the crowd. Dax held up a hand to quiet them. "And all of you are invited to our wedding which will take place—" he glanced at his watch for effect "—right now."

The excited murmurs started again as the minister from Dax's church stepped forward. Dax's sister had control of the sound system and the music changed to gentle piano by the O'Neil Brothers. A swish of recorded wind and wind chimes set a mood of peace, and hushed expectation settled on the room. As the minister began to speak and gentle strains of "I Wonder as I Wander" added background, tears filled Jenna's eyes. For indeed, she had wandered a very long distance to find her rightful place.

Dax turned to face her and spoke his words of love and commitment. His voice trembled with emotion that she knew was not nerves but his heart speaking to hers. He slid the diamond band onto her finger and then it was her turn.

She was too full of feelings to tell him everything, but she spoke from her heart, and when a tear slid down her cheek, he bent to kiss it away. A collective sigh went up from the guests.

The ceremony ended and the minister said, "Ladies and gentlemen, I present to you, Mr. and Mrs. Dax Coleman. May they always be as happy and committed as they are this moment."

Applause sounded. The photographer they had hired to capture their party and wedding snapped photo after photo. Gavin, his antlers quivering, pulled away from his grandmother and rushed to hug Dax's legs. "Does this mean Jenna is my mom now?"

Tugging Jenna down with him, Dax crouched

to meet his son at eye level. "Yep. What do you think about that?"

Gavin threw his arms around his father's neck. "I think all my Christmas wishes just came true."

As the melody of "I'll be Home for Christmas" began to play, Jenna joined the embrace of her new husband and son, thinking how prophetic both the song and Gavin's words were.

All her Christmas wishes had come true, as well, and she was truly and forever home for Christmas.

* * * * * *

This season we bring you
Christmas Treats
For an early Christmas present Linda Goodnight
would like to share a little treat with you…

Creative Way to Give Money
Teenagers love receiving money as a gift, but let's
face it, handing over an envelope of money is
kind of boring. There are many great ideas for
giving money creatively. I stumbled onto my idea
quite by accident. As I browsed the department
store, I spotted a small, inexpensive snow globe
that doubled as a two-sided photo frame, and an
idea was born. I inserted the teen's photo on one
side of the globe and a carefully folded twenty
dollar bill on the other side and wrapped the globe
as I would any other gift. When my granddaughter opened the gift and turned it over, there was
Andrew Jackson's green face smiling through the
falling snow. She loved it, of course, and can
reuse the snow globe photo frame for other
pictures. Don't have a photo of the teen? Go to
MySpace or any of the popular online commu-
nities. Chances are you can lift one there as I did.
Edible Craft for Kids
Simple, edible crafts are just the thing to get your

child involved in the Christmas celebration. One tasty and fairly healthy treat is made with pretzel rods. I've seen a number of variations, but the simplest one is pretty to look at, very tasty, and kids can make these themselves with only a little supervision. Take the fat pretzel rods and dip one end in melted almond bark/candy melt, the flavor of your choice. (I like the chocolate best, but the white chocolate and butterscotch are good, too.) Let them cool a minute and then roll in a plate of colored sprinkles, sugars, or crushed candies. The resulting product looks pretty standing in a festive cup and your child feels as if she/he has really done something special. These are great for your child to make and take to school parties, too!

0210 Rom LP

MILLS & BOON PUBLISH EIGHT LARGE PRINT TITLES A MONTH. THESE ARE THE EIGHT TITLES FOR MARCH 2010.

☙

A BRIDE FOR HIS MAJESTY'S PLEASURE
Penny Jordan

THE MASTER PLAYER
Emma Darcy

THE INFAMOUS ITALIAN'S SECRET BABY
Carole Mortimer

THE MILLIONAIRE'S CHRISTMAS WIFE
Helen Brooks

CROWNED: THE PALACE NANNY
Marion Lennox

CHRISTMAS ANGEL FOR THE BILLIONAIRE
Liz Fielding

UNDER THE BOSS'S MISTLETOE
Jessica Hart

JINGLE-BELL BABY
Linda Goodnight

MILLS & BOON PUBLISH EIGHT LARGE PRINT TITLES A MONTH. THESE ARE THE EIGHT TITLES FOR APRIL 2010.

—————————— ⟨℞⟩ ——————————

THE BILLIONAIRE'S BRIDE OF INNOCENCE
Miranda Lee

DANTE: CLAIMING HIS SECRET LOVE-CHILD
Sandra Marton

THE SHEIKH'S IMPATIENT VIRGIN
Kim Lawrence

HIS FORBIDDEN PASSION
Anne Mather

AND THE BRIDE WORE RED
Lucy Gordon

HER DESERT DREAM
Liz Fielding

THEIR CHRISTMAS FAMILY MIRACLE
Caroline Anderson

SNOWBOUND BRIDE-TO-BE
Cara Colter

millsandboon.co.uk Community

Join Us!

The Community is the perfect place to meet and chat to kindred spirits who love books and reading as much as you do, but it's also the place to:

- ■ **Get the inside scoop from authors about their latest books**
- ■ **Learn how to write a romance book with advice from our editors**
- ■ **Help us to continue publishing the best in women's fiction**
- ■ **Share your thoughts on the books we publish**
- ■ **Befriend other users**

Forums: Interact with each other as well as authors, editors and a whole host of other users worldwide.

Blogs: Every registered community member has their own blog to tell the world what they're up to and what's on their mind.

Book Challenge: We're aiming to read 5,000 books and have joined forces with The Reading Agency in our inaugural Book Challenge.

Profile Page: Showcase yourself and keep a record of your recent community activity.

Social Networking: We've added buttons at the end of every post to share via digg, Facebook, Google, Yahoo, technorati and de.licio.us.

www.millsandboon.co.uk